Cover Art © 2012 O'Neil De Noux

BOURBON street

O'NEIL DE NOUX

Dedication

I wrote this one for me and all the broken hearts along the way

Author Web Site: http://www.oneildenoux.net
Twitter: ONeilDeNoux

Published by
Big Kiss Productions
New Orleans
First Printing October 2012

Chapters

Chapter 1
YOU RUINED MY STOCKING

Desiree always wanted to be a gun-moll.

On the night she finally became one, they robbed a cattleman from Topeka, leaving him in his undershirt and skivvies along Highway 90, just this side of The Rigolets Pass, the narrows separating Lake Pontchartrain from Lake Borgne. As they sped away in Bogarde's gray Ford coupe with its license plate removed, Desiree looked back at the mark and said, "He'll be eaten alive by mosquitoes."

Bogarde laughed so hard he almost drove off the narrow highway. "We rob the bastard and you're worried about mosquitoes."

"I'm allergic to mosquitoes, mister smarty-pants. I get welts the size of quarters." Desiree turned back around and straightened her dress. The cattleman, whose name was Elmer, had been pawing her, fumbling with the zipper of her new Christian Dior when Bogarde climbed out of the trunk with his forty-five. Dark red, the dress was part of the 'new look' for 1947, a return to the classic feminine 'nipped waist' as the salesman at D. H. Holmes had explained. It was the latest fashion from Paris with a tight waist, big circular skirt and snug bodice which Desiree had to re-fasten as Bogarde zipped the Ford back to the city.

"Better slow down," she said as she finished straightening herself. "And take off that silly mask. All we need is to get pulled over by the cops. You haven't even put the license plate back on."

Bogarde peeled off the gorilla mask and sneered at her. "Cops got better things to do that patrol out here. You OK?"

"Yes," she snapped and tried to control her heavy breathing. Her neck felt flushed and her body tingled with, of all things, sexual excitement. She could barely sit still. What they had just done, the actual stick-up had lit a simmering fire inside Desiree. She felt as if she were on a roller-coaster barreling down the side of a mountain.

She looked at the road. The tall trees on either side gave the road a tunnel effect. In the moonlight, Desiree could make out water beyond the trees on their left. On their right lay a huge cypress swamp, its sickly, musty smell rich in the air. She leaned away from the seat, her back damp with perspiration, sweaty in the middle of the night. It was much hotter down here than back in Wayne County, north Mississippi. She didn't think anything could be hotter than summer in Wayne County until she came to New Orleans where the air was so much thicker, the humidity like steam rising from a boiling pot. She hated the heat.

Bogarde turned on the interior light and said, "Count the take."

Desiree opened the mark's wallet and scooped out the bills, spotting a hundred dollar bill immediately. Bogarde let out an impatient growl. "The money belt, Babe. Check the money belt."

"Wallet first." Desiree's heart raced as she fanned through the bills. Besides the Ben Franklin, there were two Grants, two Andy Jacksons, two Abe Lincolns and two Washingtons. Two fifty-two, not bad at all. She unzipped the money belt and her heart stammered. Nothing but Franklins. She counted them twice, her hands shaking. Five grand in the belt.

"Sweet Jesus!" said Bogarde. They passed a couple fishing camps on creosote stilts, one with lights still on at three o'clock in the morning. Bogarde flipped off the interior light. Desiree rubbed a crisp Franklin between her fingers, feeling its embossed texture. She lifted the bill and sniffed it. She crinkled it, getting excited, breathing heavier now.

"Knew that bastard was loaded," Bogarde said. "Probably even more in his hotel room."

Desiree felt her stomach flip-flop. "I still don't think it's a good idea going to his hotel in the middle of the night. I mean, we'll be seen."

"You'll be seen." Bogarde turned his green eyes to her and gave her the look. He called it his hypnotic stare, managing to open his eyes wide while furrowing his brow. When he first gave Desiree the look three months ago, she felt as if his eyes actually touched her. Tonight, he looked like a bad actor trying to impersonate Bela Lugosi's Dracula stare. If she wasn't so juiced-up, she'd giggle.

"What did I tell you?" Bogarde went. "Let me do the thinking. You do what you do best. Look sexy." He gave her a wicked grin.

"Now put the money away and toss out the wallet and money belt."

"Gimme the mask too."

"No way." He tossed the mask to the back seat. "It's our M.O. We're the 'beauty-and-the-beast gang'."

Jesus – she thought – he got the second part right.

She waited for another swampy area to toss both out. Then she dug the compact and lipstick out of her purse, turned on the interior light again to touch up her lips. No time for contouring, she'd just reapply the crimson lipstick. Normally Desiree painted her lips as carefully as an artist, using several shades of lipstick, starting with pink, moving on to scarlet, topping it off with a deep crimson red that made her lips jump out.

Bogarde laughed aloud. "Man, ole Elmer look like a freakin' retard standing there in his drawers."

Desiree nodded as she finished the lipstick, thinking most men looked like retards in their drawers. Desiree Blanc was twenty-five with ash-blond hair cut in a long page boy. Her sky blue eyes seemed a little large for her thin face. She considered her lips her best feature, sculptured lips, the upper lip rising to a slight point, the lower lip a little fuller, both looking dazzling in bright red lipstick. She knew she had a pretty face, but men didn't consider it, nor her lips for that matter, or her sky blue eyes when they looked at her. Her breasts attracted their attention. C-cup tits on a slim frame immediately drew most male eyes. At five-ten, Desiree stood as tall as six foot Bogarde when she was in heels, like tonight. She'd towered over Elmer the cattleman.

Last summer, when she'd strolled into the Hotsy Jazz Club in the five hundred block of Bourbon Street, Fat Sal Cardona tried to act nonchalant as he gave her a good look up and down and said, "Yeah. You could be a stripper." That brought chuckles from the two men in the joint.

Fat Sal led her to his office at the rear of the place, a room with black walls, a beat-up desk and an orange sofa in front of the desk. The room smelled of mildew, B.O. and stale smoke. Sitting behind his desk, Fat Sal wore a tennis shirt two sizes too small and pants that hung well beneath his belly. He sucked on a thick cigar that smelled like rotten wood.

They passed the hotel parking lot and Desiree looked up at the brown brick building. About a dozen stories tall with large concrete pots on either side of the doorway just below the large name in some sort of a Chinese script: Jung. Bogarde stopped the car to synchronize their watches.

"I don't have a watch."

He huffed. "Gimme five minutes to park the car and go in the side door."

"Don't forget to put the license plate back on."

He huffed again. "Better let me take the money."

"I don't think so. You might get caught in there."

"I'll leave it in the car."

"Your car got stolen last month, remember?"

Desiree got out quickly, the money safe in her purse. Bogarde sat with his mouth open a few moments before taking off and turning up the side street. LaSalle Street she noted as she stepped up to the front doors. A young night clerk behind the desk was reading a magazine. She remained outside, her back to the glass door, and stood there as if waiting for someone. He might notice, but wouldn't see her face.

She counted the seconds. After three minutes, she decided she'd put on a little show after all. If the guy was watching her through the doors he'd see her pull up her stockings as Bogarde slipped into the side entrance, straight to the elevators. Another two minutes and she heard the door open behind her.

"Can I help you ma'am?"

She waved over her shoulder as she moved away. "Nope, here comes my streetcar."

Desiree tip-toed across wet Canal Street to the wide median New Orleanians call a neutral ground running down the center of the widest main street in America, according to the tourist brochures put out by the city. As the streetcar slowly lumbered her way, Desiree glanced back at the Jung. The night clerk had gone back inside. She waited for the streetcar to get closer, seeing it was almost empty, before crossing to the other side of Canal to move with the streetcar shielding her from the Jung. She headed for Wit's End Diner, where Bogarde was supposed to pick her up exactly a half hour after he'd dropped her off. The wooden streetcar threw electric sparks from its overhead wires as it crossed the intersection of LaSalle.

'Refrigerated Air' was painted across the picture window of the all-night diner. Black script with icicles dripping from the letters. It was cool inside. Mixed with the moist air and Desiree's damp dress, it made her shiver as she entered. Finally, a relief from the heat. She felt the weight of the money when she switched her purse from one shoulder to the other, her heartbeat rising again with just the thought.

The Negro cook behind the grill checked her out, but not obviously. He wasn't about to stare too long at a white woman. A lone customer sat in a booth with his back to the door, the lone waitress on a stool at the counter. Beehive hair about a foot tall, the heavy-set waitress thumbed through a film magazine as Desiree passed to the rear booth. As she sat, the lone customer looked up from his coffee and Desiree felt her stomach flip-flop again. Damn her luck, his face was familiar.

He looked away quickly as she slid on the bench-seat to the window. The waitress came with a short glass of water and a menu, which Desiree didn't look at.

"Coffee."

"We got fresh pecan pie, apple too."

Desiree's stomach was too jittery to eat anything. She stuck with the coffee.

A delicious smell of meat cooking wafted through the diner and Desiree watched the cook slip two pork chops on a plate, which the waitress took to the familiar-faced guy who was staring at Desiree now. A wary smile came to his face as he raised his right hand and hesitantly waved.

My God, he was one of the bar-backs at Hotsy Jazz, quiet guy, never a vulgar remark, never leering at her when he watched her strip. He was the young guy with the limp who kept to himself. She watched him cut up a pork chop, him not looking at her now. He seemed a little embarrassed.

The waitress brought her coffee. "Sorry it took a minute. Made a fresh pot."

"Thanks." Desiree picked up her purse, the cup and saucer and went to the booth where the bar-back sat. He looked up at her with eyes so dark brown, they were almost black. He sported a two-day beard that gave his face a hint of danger. She liked it, especially on a square-jawed man.

"Mind if I sit with you?" This would shake up Mr. Overconfident Bogarde. God, Desiree's heart was flying.

He nodded slowly, those eyes telling her he couldn't believe she's just said that. In a deep voice, he said, "I like what you did with your hair, Miss Blanc."

Desiree slipped into the booth across from him, smiled and used a line she's seen in movies but never had the opportunity to say, until that moment. "You have the advantage of me."

A shy smile curled his lips as he said, "Jim Munster."

"Well, Jim Munster, what brings you out in the middle of the night?"

"I have the same days off as you. This is my normal lunch hour time."

That's right. He worked midnights. She'd only seen him at the end of her shift because he came in early. She worked four to midnight.

"Just came from a midnight movie. *Dark Passage* with Bogie and Bacall."

Desiree smiled. "Gotta love those two together. Was it as good as *The Big Sleep*?"

"Well, no, but ... but it was different. Bogart on the run, gets plastic surgery and falls for Bacall."

A loud popping outside caused Desiree to spill her coffee as it was about to reach her lips.

"Was that a gun?"

Jim leaned over with his napkin to wipe the spilled coffee from the table in front of her and spoke with his head down, "Fireworks. Sounded like cherry bombs." He looked up with those brown eyes, close now. "It *is* the Fourth of July."

Desiree's hand was shaking too much to raise the coffee cup again. She took in a deep breath. "What was I talking about?"

"Movies." He leaned back and took a sip of his coffee.

"Oh. Yeah. Never forget *To Have and Have Not*, the way she came on to him. Kissing him just to see what it was like." Why was she so nervous? Chattering like that. Desiree patted her purse next to her, reassured it was there safe and full of money.

Bogarde took that moment to rush in, stopping immediately. The look on his face was priceless. Mr. Oh-so-cool was stunned seeing her sitting with another man. Desiree was glad she caught the look because it only lasted a moment before he straightened and walked casually over.

"Hey, Babe," he said as he arrived. "The tire's fixed. We can go."

"You found a filing station open at this time in the morning?"

His eyes bulged.

Desiree took a sip of coffee, hands no longer shaking. "This is Jim Munster. He works at Hotsy Jazz. One of the bar-backs."

Jim looked up at Bogarde and stuck out his hand to shake. The men shook hands a little longer than usual. One of those dumb test-of-strength handshakes. Bogarde narrowed his left eye and folded his arms.

"Yeah. I seen you at Hotsy. Club foot, right?"

Desiree blanched.

Jim looked back at her. "It's not a club foot." He lifted his coffee to his lips. "It was a gift from the Wehrmacht during the little ditty they called the Wacht am Rhein Offensive." He took a sip.

"The what?" Desiree asked.

"We called it the Battle of the Bulge." Jim looked up at Bogarde again. "What'd you do during the war?"

Bogarde gave him a long stare, reached slowly for Desiree's shoulder and said, "Come on, Babe. We gotta go."

She slid over, dragging the purse with her. Bogarde took her hand. Jim slid out too and told her it was nice seeing her away from work. Bogarde squeezed her hand and said, "Yeah, well don't make a habit of it, Slick."

Jim Munster was about five-ten, only a couple inches shorter than Bogarde, but huskier, shoulders much wider. He gave Desiree a shy smile and nodded as he sat back down and forked a piece of pork chop.

Desiree paid for the coffee while Bogarde impatiently held the diner's door open. On their way across Canal Street, Bogarde growled, "Goddamn cripple givin' me that 'what did you do during the war' horse crap. Like he won the war all by himself."

She waited until they were getting in the car, Bogarde on the other side before she asked, "You didn't take long. Did you get in the room?"

"None of the damn keys worked."

She didn't want to tell him again, the keys on Elmer's key chain didn't look like hotel room keys. They were usually on a separate ring with a wooden disk. Guests usually left them at the front desk. Bogarde started the engine and Desiree wondered – if she didn't have the money in her purse – he may not reach over and unlock the door, which he did, eventually.

• • •

Bogarde found a parking spot right in front of his apartment house on Burgundy Street. The building used to be a hotel, still had a faint outline of its name above the front door: Hotel L'Acteur. It was a two-story masonry building with some of the masonry worn away to reveal the red bricks-between-wood beam construction. Its green paint had faded badly but Bogarde's apartment, on the second floor overlooking the street, was fairly clean with hardwood floors. What it could use was a rug or two.

The living room was almost cool with the ceiling fans turning and the windows cracked. The room smelled like cooked spaghetti, which Bogarde never seemed to notice. The Italian family in the next apartment were always cooking and yelling. Bogarde took Desiree's hand and pulled her toward the sofa, his free hand grabbing her ass.

"Wait. You'll tear my dress."

"I'll buy you another."

"No you won't." She pulled away and started unzipping the Dior. Bogarde plopped on the sofa, reaching over to pull her purse to him. By the time Desiree was down to her bra and panties, he had the money laid out on the small coffee table.

Her heartbeat rose as she looked down at the stoic face of Ben Franklin.

"Good haul," said Bogarde as he stood and unbuttoned his shirt.

Desiree headed to the bedroom.

"No. Out here," he called out. He liked it on the sofa, which was too damn uncomfortable.

"I'll be in here," she said, dropping bra and panties and climbing on the cool bed sheets. Bogarde didn't come in right away, probably trying to out-wait her, but she could wait. Eventually he came in naked, moving straight for her.

"Rubber," she called out. He sighed but went to the nightstand and put one on.

It was pretty frenzied, both juiced up from the dough, she figured. Bogarde kissed his way down her body from her mouth, all the way down – to do what he did best. After giving her pleasure, he climbed atop her to get his. Quickly. She expected more from the excitement she'd felt earlier but the sex was fairly mechanical.

Lying face up, both caught their breaths while the ceiling fan worked to cool their bodies. Desiree didn't want to fall asleep and fought it. Bogarde's easy breathing told her he was drifting.

"What *did* you during the war?" she whispered.

"I was a guest … of the great state of Illinois." His voice a faint whisper.

"You were in jail?"

She thought he'd fallen asleep or just wasn't going to answer before he said, "It was a lot tougher to survive … than the army."

Desiree felt a lump in her belly. She shouldn't let it shake her, she told herself, because she was a gun-moll and gun-molls slept with gangsters. But maybe it was the way he'd said it, so casually. With her eyes closed she could see Jim Munster limping around Hotsy Jazz. The war was over, she told herself. But who was she kidding? If it wasn't for Munster and so many others, where would they be now?

She lay there until Bogarde starting snoring, got up and washed before getting back into her clothes. Sitting on the sofa, she counted the take again and spilt it down the middle, twenty-six hundred and twenty-six bucks each, stuffing her cut into the purse before slipping out of the apartment.

The air was thick with humidity, still steamy with dawn not far away. Desiree moved down the dark street, heading for the yellowish streetlight at the end of the block, heels echoing off the banquette. She looked around as she moved and thought of the quaint, New Orleans term, 'banquette', what they called sidewalks down here because they were raised to allow the streets to flood. They were banks to walk on while rainwater filled the streets.

She passed a dark playground just before Barracks Street, watching as a gray DeSoto cruised slowly past. The dark-haired driver gave her a look as he went by, but revealed nothing on his face. Probably a detective. She watched the car go up to Esplanade Avenue and turn right.

When she got to Esplanade, she crossed to the neutral ground and moved through the tall oaks down the avenue. The thick air reeked with the musty scent of tree bark. A white milk truck passed up the avenue but there was no one out on the stoops of the smaller houses or the big front porches of the mansions along the avenue. Fireworks echoed behind her in the distance.

At Chartres Street she crossed the avenue in front of an approaching car, which stopped immediately and she saw it was a two-man black prowl car, a white New Orleans Police star-and-crescent badge on its door. The car stopped. She felt the weight of the Franklins in her purse as she switched it from her right shoulder to the left.

Gun-moll. She was a gun-moll, her heart racing again as she looked back at the nearest patrolman in his light blue police shirt, elbow sticking out the window. If she ignored them completely, they would be suspicious. She rolled her shoulders slightly as she passed and gave the patrolman a wink.

He gave her a lingering, greedy stare. She felt them watching her as she continued down Chartres and let out a breath when she didn't hear them following. Two short blocks later, she took a quick left on Frenchmen Street to her boarding house.

There was time for a shower before breakfast and Desiree didn't like to miss one of Mrs. Watson's breakfasts. As she ascended the stairs to the third floor, she remembered the day she'd found the place. The building had been converted from a single family mansion into nine apartments, the Watson House. It was a cut above any boarding house in the Quarter.

Chubby Mrs. Watson had apologized that the room was all the way at the top as she breathed heavily going up the stairs. "But you have you own private bath," the old woman added as she led Desiree into what once was an attic, but had been decorated into a comfortable bedroom. Small, but clean.

"What do you do, young lady?" Mrs. Watson had asked.

"I'm a dancer."

"Bourbon Street?"

"Yes, ma'am." No sense in lying.

"You have the dearest Mississippi accent," Mrs. Watson said. "Don't lose it. New Orleans people sound like they're from Brooklyn. Do you strip?"

"Um ..."

"Well, you should. You seem to have a lovely figure and men should pay to see it. Make all the money you can while you can, then get out of town."

The room overlooked a small bricked back yard with vines and exotic plants, banana, and long pointy rubber plants. Desiree had a small balcony and usually kept the French doors cracked to let in night air. She dropped her purse on the bed, went out on the balcony and watched the faint sunlight slowly draw the rooftops into a soft impressionist view.

Twenty-six hundred and twenty-six bucks. Not a bad take her first outing as a gun-moll.

Desiree closed her eyes as a light breeze came in from the river, a breeze thick with the scent of the muddy Mississippi. She closed her right hand slowly and could almost feel the wooden grip of the forty-five in her hand, the way it felt smooth and warm as she pointed it at Elmer while Bogarde took the mark's wallet and money belt. Her finger quivered on the trigger, her mouth dry as the Sahara, the rush of adrenaline pulsing through her veins.

Damn, it felt so good, so evil and so powerful, holding that gun, robbing that mark. The tingling returned and her neck flushed once more. She felt lust rising and knew she had to do it all again, as soon as possible.

She *was* a gun-moll.

Her eyes snapped open and she let out a little squeal.

Two thousand, six hundred and twenty-six bucks. Anyway you put it sounded heavenly.

Chapter 2
I LIKE IT FINE

Abraham Lincoln Bogarde knew one thing for sure – the world was full of chumps. Just like Elmer, the fool from Topeka. As he shaved before heading to work, Bogarde – he preferred using his last name because who the hell wanted to be called 'Abraham' or worse, 'Abe' – ran the events of the previous evening through his mind. He nicked himself when he thought of the money lying on the coffee table.

Damn chippy actually took half the take. *Half.* Man-o-man, he was going to have to show her there was only one person wearing the pants in this gang and it was him. He winked at himself in the mirror. Abraham Lincoln Bogarde stood six feet even and weighed about ten pounds more than he'd weighed in high school. Light brown hair, wavy up top, added to his debonair appearance. At thirty, he could pass for a twenty year old, if needed. But it was his green eyes that set him apart from mere mortals, as he liked to say.

Light green eyes, pale green, with specks of gold dotting the irises, his were hypnotic eyes. Bogarde had practiced for years to perfect the hypnotic stare, drawing women like bits of iron to a magnet. His eyes were mesmerizing. They'd taken in Desiree so easily, just as they'd taken the older women he ran around with, women with money, lonely women made happy by Bogarde, before he moved on.

He glanced at the electric clock. Nine a.m. He had an hour.

Splashing after-shave on his face, he powdered his body before climbing into boxers, pulling up calf-high socks before pulling on an undershirt. Today he wore the same nifty outfit he'd seen on the Duke of Windsor, a picture in *Argosy*. He climbed into coral slacks, a crisp white shirt, a sea green ascot and tan loafers. The Duke never looked this good. What? Ho? As the Brits say.

Bogarde put the money away, shoving it into an empty coffee can in the cupboard, before grabbing his tan fedora and going out into the bright sunlight. He had time for breakfast. He slipped on his new aviator sunglasses as he breezed down Burgundy Street. Passing run-down Creole cottages and wooden shotgun houses, he tried not to notice the seamy side of the lower French Quarter. He ignored depressing things, like ugly people, fat women, homely kids and working-class men with no class. He chuckled to himself because Desiree thought he'd done hard time in Joliet, as if he was a hardened criminal. Bogarde had done a short stint in Joliet during the war but it was for hot-wiring cars in Chicago and selling them in Cairo, Illinois. He never carried a gun and never got in any shootouts like he'd told Desiree when they first met.

There were no pretty women for Bogarde to ogle on his way to the new Arabesque Café, corner of Burgundy and Barracks Streets, caddie-corner from Cabrini Playground. He glanced at the magnolias and oaks in the park. There were no women lingering in the park, only two boys tossing a raggedy football.

The waitress at the café was homely, thick bodied with dark, Mediterranean skin, probably Greek or Turkish, certainly not his type. Sitting at an outside table on the banquette, Bogarde used a little of his abundant charm on the waitress, getting her to blush by focusing his mesmerizing eyes on her for a lingering moment.

He took Turkish coffee with his breakfast roll, sat nibbling the roll and sipping the strong coffee, smelling bananas now from the wharves a few blocks away, and thought of Desiree. She was gorgeous, no doubt about it, and a willing partner, sexually and in his new criminal endeavors. She was a great piece when she put her mind and ass into it. And she had the greatest rack he'd ever seen and he'd seen a lotta tits. Gravity-defying, poking straight out with those small pink nipples and light pink areoles – she'd taught him that word.

But she had a flippant side, a smart-aleck side, as if she was as smart as Bogarde. And what was that crap with the bar-back last night in the cafe? She was pulling his string and no dame did that.

Maybe he should start calling her by her real name – Dorothy Jellnick. What was the name of the place she was from in redneck Mississippi? Wolf's Howl or Wolf Bark? Hell, there hadn't been wolves in Mississippi since God knew when. She'd told him about growing up dirt poor, an orchid sprouted from hillbilly weeds, how everyone and she said *everyone* in the entire county couldn't believe how pretty she was and that she should go to Hollywood and show them real southern beauty. She got as far west as Bourbon Street.

Bogarde finished off his roll, downed the last of the coffee, gave the waitress a salacious wink in lieu of a decent tip and waltzed up to the streetcar on Rampart Street to get over to Canal Street in time for work. He got two women to blush as the electric streetcar rattled its way up Canal.

As soon as he spotted Z Best Cars, corner Canal and Galvez Street, his heart sank. His boss had attached red, white and blue balloons to the antennas of every used car on the lot. More depressing was the sight of his boss, standing with his hands on his hips. James Bowyer, who insisted on being called Jiminy, as in Jiminy Cricket, was an albino, standing six-three, skinny as a stove-pipe, his white hair cut in crew-cut. He wore his blue seersucker suit today with a bright red tie, white shirt and white shoes.

First thing out of his mouth to Bogarde was, "Why aren't you in red, white and blue?" Then he handed Bogarde a top hat decorated with stars-and-stripes to wear because it was Independence Day and they already had two couples cruising the lot.

"Go on," Jiminy said. "It's a holiday. They don't come on the lot if they don't wanna buy somethin'."

Chump. Jiminy Bowyer was such a goddamn chump. Bogarde exchanged his fedora for the top hat, trying not to mess up his hair too much, and headed for the nearest couple, replaying his daydream of taking Jiminy out to Lake Catherine and putting two in the back of the bastard's head. He'd played out the scene so many times, slapping Jiminy so hard the pink eyes would cross, yanking him by the hair as he dragged the bastard to the edge of the water, having him kneel there, then pressing the forty-five against the back of Jiminy's pointed head.

"Know why I'm doing this?" he would growl.

Jiminy would only whimper in response.

"Because I can." And Bogarde would pull the trigger twice, quickly, feeling the heavy gun recoil, smelling the gunpowder and the scent of fresh blood as Jiminy flopped in the mud like a speared catfish for a good three seconds before lying still. It would be right at sundown and Bogarde wouldn't have to wait long for the first gator, drawn by the blood, to come and feast.

"So," Bogarde called out to the portly couple checking out a '36 Buick. "I see I have someone who knows cars."

The man stood about five-five, soft looking with a jowly, pallid face. He wore a neatly pressed brown suit and black shoes. The woman, as wide as she was tall, came around the car and said, "Doris and Donald Chitchester." She wore a pink chiffon dress with baby blue high heels. "Is this the model with the RCA Deluxe radio?"

Hell if I know – thought Bogarde, but actually said, "Well, let's see."

The radio was an RCA. Doris climbed in, settling her big butt on the seat and said, "Buick Century, four passenger convertible coupe. It retailed for $1135 back in Thirty-six. One hundred and twenty horsepower, this one should have a straight-eight cylinder. Let's pop the hood."

It was the easiest sale of the day, although Doris picked on the two small dents in the rear bumper and tried to get the price down, but the Century was one of the best cars on the lot, all pre-war of course, and Bogarde made the sale.

Bogarde watched the Chitchesters drive off, took off his hat and wiped his brow as a string of fire-crackers popped across the narrow side street running off Canal Street.

"You goddamn delinquents!" screeched Jiminy in his high-pitched voice as some kids ran off. "You damage my cars and I'll sue your parents into the poor house!"

Bogarde looked at his Bulova watch. Only seven hours to go. *Jesus*.

• • •

Always on the lookout for next mark, Bogarde checked out everyone who came on the car lot. Few would be as easy as Elmer, coming around tugging up his money belt as he casually looked at a '32 Cadillac. Jiminy helped him. Moron couldn't tell Elmer was just slumming. That was when Bogarde spotted Elmer pulling up his money belt. Elmer told them where he was staying and how he much he loved New Orleans 'cause of the pretty women. How the women 'gussied' themselves up down here. He liked walking along Canal Street, hawking out the girls. When Bogarde told Desiree the story, she'd come up with the bump and fall idea.

At exactly six p.m., Bogarde tossed his top hat to Jiminy, who opened his big mouth to say something but didn't. Bogarde had sold the only cars that day, three to be exact. He hustled to catch a passing streetcar going up Canal and took it all the way to the cemeteries.

Chippy Number Two lived in a two story house behind Odd Fellow's Rest Cemetery at the end of Canal Street. She rented the downstairs to a couple newly arrived from Cuba and lived upstairs. Bogarde took the concrete steps two at a time and found Chippy Number Two sitting on the porch swing, a high ball in her left hand. Her name was Fanny Depardieu, of Creole French descent as she often told him – "My Great Granddaddy opened the first woman's dress store in the Quarter long before you Americans came."

Depardieu's Department Store, corner Canal and Rampart Streets, still stood, although there were new owners. Yankees from Boston.

Fanny gave Bogarde a bored look, said, "Why is that man always a jack-ass when I call?"

She'd called three times and Jiminy had hung up on her, snapping at Bogarde about broads always calling him at work. "It's always broads with you. You need to settle down, start a family."

Jesus Christ. Jiminy was married to a human version of one of those stick insects. She looked like a Dachau survivor. A real shrew with a profusion for profanity that would astonish a sailor, Matlida Bowyer disliked Bogarde so much she wouldn't talk to him, which pleased him immensely. She's actually tried to flirt with him when he was first hired at Z Best Cars, but he rebuffed her so the woman's scorn was focused on him. Jiminy said she'd tried to get him to fire Bogarde but he wore the pants in their family.

Yeah? No way he'd fire his best salesman, especially after Desiree breezed in for a visit some weeks ago. She wore a tight red blouse and white shorts, flashing that fake-shy smile, batting those blue eyes at Jiminy as she rolled her shoulders. She had that move down pat.

"You wanna high ball?" asked Fanny as Bogarde sat next to her on the wooden swing, suspended on chains from the overhang.

He stroked the side of Fanny's neck and said, "What I want is you."

She pinched his side with her free hand and said, "Calm down, boy. I've got a pork roast in the oven, candied yams, a loaf of Italian ciabatta bread ready to pop in the oven and my grandmother's special made pecan pie for dessert."

He nibbled her neck and purred, "You'll be my dessert."

Fanny Depardieu was forty-three but told everyone she was thirty-five. Bogarde found her driver's license when he was rifling her purse on their first evening together. A war widow, her husband died on one of those Pacific islands with a funny name. She'd told Bogarde the story but he purposefully forgot the name of the island. Mr. Depardieu was a marine or one of those navy Seabee guys.

Fanny wasn't heavy but she was a long way from skinny. She was a full-figured gal with dark brown hair, dark brown eyes and a great fanny which she rolled at him as she moved away from the swing into her living room. What else could he do but follow, all the way to the kitchen where she was bent over the stove. He grabbed that fanny and squeezed.

"Don't! I'm basting. Fix yourself a drink."

He didn't go back out to the bar in the living room, opting for a cold Schlitz from the fridge.

"Can't believe you had to work on the Fourth of July." Fanny put on an apron and took a hit of her high ball. "Go out in the living room and listen to the radio while I warm this loaf in the oven."

Bogarde went to the Victrola and found Benny Goodman tooting his clarinet. He moved to the front windows to look across the street at another two-story house, this one occupied by a future mark. James Gallagher, manager of the Chartres National Bank, married to a librarian, father of two, was a patron of Hotsy Jazz where he wore a fake moustache. The man was smitten by Desiree who didn't even notice him.

The beginning of a plan was forming in Bogarde's mind. He sensed this chump could be taken for good money. They had to be careful of course. Unlike Elmer, who didn't know Desiree and only saw Bogarde in the background at the car lot, James Gallagher knew exactly where to find Desiree.

So far, what he'd come up with – and he hadn't run it by Desiree yet – was for her to let the stiff put a move on her. Maybe go to bed with him. Bogarde in the closet taking pictures. Blackmail never worked but maybe she and Bogarde could visit the bank, talk the stiff into letting them see the vault and sticking up the bank from the inside. To hell with the tellers. Clean out the vault and ole James Gallagher couldn't finger Desiree because if he did, the photos would come out and he'd be ruined. Hell, the bank's money was insured. It just might work.

Bogarde took another hit of Schlitz and smiled to himself.

"Supper's on," Fanny called out.

"I'm coming."

For the next half hour, Bogarde endured Fanny's gossip about her neighbors, as if he gave a rat's ass that Myrtle's husband bought her a new Dodge or that the neighborhood bum, who slept under the railroad overpass by City Park, was being awfully cozy with the widow Dietz or those ruffians who kept playing football in the street when City Park was only blocks away.

The difference with Fanny in bed was the way she reached for it, like a hungry lioness. Sometimes it was too much, even for Bogarde, watching her face scrunch up as they made love. Desiree became even more beautiful when they screwed. Fanny got scrunchy and bounced like they were on a bed of hot coals. After sex, Desiree like to cuddle. Fanny acted as if she'd just been recharged, chattering incessantly, getting up to dust, even vacuuming the house while he tried to get some shut eye.

"That was a good one," she said. "You're such an attentive lover."

Attentive? He was counting the money they'd scored from Elmer over and over again. And just as he was slipping away, she bounded out of bed and said, "Come on. We have time for a shower before the fireworks display in City Park tonight."

• • •

The sharp pain in his mouth throbbed and he knew he'd bitten his tongue but that wasn't the problem. The trees exploding was the problem, jagged splinters of bark and wood zipping around him, tearing at his fatigues as he tried to push his way through the earth all the way to China. He'd lost his hearing at the start of the German bombardment, but felt the concussions in his bones.

Jim Munster knew he was dreaming but couldn't stop. This dream wasn't even the day his foot was mangled in a forest called the Ardennes. This was another battle, an earlier battle, a far worse battle for the First Infantry Division. It was in a different forest, the Hürtgen, where Jim's platoon suffered a ninety-percent casualty rate.

The dream was in slow motion and he saw himself, not through his eyes, but the eyes of another trooper, as the bombardment stopped and smoky fog circled. He saw himself stand on unsteady legs and urge the men forward and they stumbled and screamed headlong into the entrenched Germans, Jim spitting blood from his tongue as he bayoneted a Nazi grenadier, then cut down others with the M1 rifle he'd picked up on the battlefield after his captured Karabiner 98k sniper rifle, the one he'd used since Oran, had been blown apart by shrapnel. They routed the Nazis, then collapsed in the trenches and waited for darkness.

His dream played out, how he'd read about that day, about that forgotten battle because shortly after came the Battle of the Bulge, which stole the spotlight. He remembered reading in the papers about the Battle of the Hürtgen Forest, the longest single battle the US Army ever fought, how the brain-trust at headquarters thought we needed to remove the threat of the Germans blowing up the Ruhr River dam to slow the US advance and the quickest route to the dam was through the thick forest. Ernest Hemingway, who was there, called the battle, "Passchendaele with tree bursts," likening the Hürtgen to that most horrific of World War I battles.

It wasn't biting his tongue that woke Jim, it was the popping sound of gunfire. Opening his eyes to the stained ceiling over his bed, feeling the dampness of his sheets, it took a second to realize it wasn't gunfire but firecrackers. The Fourth of July. He looked at the small electric clock next to his bed and it was almost six p.m.

Jim Munster struggled from bed and began his ritual, getting to his feet and limping over to the sink for aspirin and water. He downed four aspirins and looked at his bruised tongue in the mirror, no blood but he'd bitten it hard this time. He stood with his hands gripping the sink and slowly worked his left foot as much as he could. Sharp pain shot up his leg and for a moment he thought of reaching for the pain killers the VA doctors gave him, but they dulled his senses too much and he had to work tonight.

He moved back to the bed, sat and drew his left foot up to massage it, feeling needles sticking it as the pain increased. He shut his eyes tightly and thought of Desiree coming out of the rain into the café and the way those lake-blue eyes looked back at him, a gleam in them as if she really enjoyed sitting there with him. The image of that white hot body of hers in that red dress, catching the outline of busts pressed against the soft material of the dress, the same naked breasts he'd seen as she slowly danced at Hotsy Jazz raised his heart rate. Desiree did everything in slow motion when she stripped, dragging it out, drawing the attention. The other strippers bounced and twirled in quick circles, but Desiree brought it out a little at a time and let everyone have a nice long look at her naked body with only a g-string and two pasties over her nipples, that ash blond hair glowing in the subdued light.

Desiree had no blemishes on her pallid flesh, no tan lines, her skin glimmered like white satin, her face seeming to glow when she stripped, letting the men pant as they leered at her. Then she went off-stage and rarely came back out to sit with the customers, like most of the other girls. Then again, Jim only saw Desiree when he came in early or she worked overtime, since she worked four-to-midnight and he worked midnight-to-eight a.m.

Thinking of the way Desiree looked at him, right into his eye, it feeling like an electric pull as her eyes looked at his. It was as if they were smiling, as if she liked him, not romantically, but maybe as a friend. She certainly never gave him that vacant, bored look the other girls gave the help at Hotsy.

The stiff she was with last night, he'd seen before. The guy was smarmy, a slick bastard who thought he was tough but looked to be about half-a-left hook. That's all it would take to floor the bastard and Jim was itching to do it, even before he knew the bastard had linked up with Desiree. Some people you just hate from the moment you see them.

It took a half hour of painful manipulations to get the ankle to bend at all. Walking on it, still painful, did limber it up somewhat. Jim took a quick, cool shower, threw on a tee-shirt and dungarees and headed out. The Creole cottage he lived in, renting the left side while his landlady occupied the right was of original French construction, built of brick-between-cypress beams with a masonry covering. It was painted a pale green and had a wooden front porch, little more than a stoop, where the landlady, Mrs. O'Keefe, usually sat perched as she gossiped with neighbors in the early evening, when the sun wasn't so brutal and just before the mosquitoes assembled for their evening attack.

A half dozen boys, with two girls watching, set off a string of firecrackers down at the corner of Marigny and Royal Streets. He watched them as he passed, watched the boys show off for the girls, shouting and bouncing around while the girls played coy.

He turned up Royal over to Elysian Fields and bought the evening paper from a newsstand. The headline read: Truman Rejects Soviet Charge. He glanced at the story. Apparently the benevolent Soviet Union claimed the Marshall Plan was 'divisive'. Yeah, because you're not getting any aid, freakin' bloodsuckers.

A half block up, Jim stepped into Tantillo's, a small, family restaurant occupying the bottom of a two-story wooden building with a balcony out front and gingerbread trim. It was dark inside from soft yellow lights and cool air-conditioned air washed over him, along with the rich scents of pasta and tomato gravy. Mama Tantillo sat at the register near the front door, while her daughters Maria and Luiga worked the eight tables. Papa Tantillo was the cook. It was a little early for the supper rush, only three other customers, so Jim had his pick of tables and chose one by the front window. Maria brought him a menu and ice water, placing them on the red checker table cloth and nodding, *"Buona sera."*

"Buona sera," he said back, knowing it meant 'good evening'.

Maria and Luiga were large women, younger than Jim, both married with kids. The sisters smiled a lot and were good servers. Even better than the service was the food at Tantillo's. Without looking at the menu, Jim ordered an espresso and pane.

He noticed one of the customers moving his way and looked up at a face he knew. It didn't smile but the eyes narrowed and the man nodded, pulling a chair out from Jim's table and sitting without invitation.

"Senoré Alphonso," Jim said.

"Al," said the man. "How's it going, son?"

Alphonso Badalamente wasn't old enough to call Jim 'son'. He was around Jim's age, twenty-six, but seemed older. A burly man with a wide face, a thick mane of wavy black hair and a thick moustache, Alphonso was olive skinned with eyes almost black, like a shark's eyes. He didn't blink much, which was disconcerting.

Maria brought Jim his espresso and pane and slipped an espresso in front of Badalamente who nodded in appreciation and began adding sugar to his.

"It's Jim, isn't it?"

"Yes, it is."

"How you like working at Hotsy?"

"I like it fine."

The shark eyes stared at Jim but held no expression.

"I watch you work when you don't think I watch you work and you're hard worker. Fat Sal treatin' you OK?"

"Yes, sir."

"Sal says a lotta stupid things, but long as he treats you OK." Badalamente peeked around the table at Jim's left leg. "That's a war wound right? You're a vet."

Jim nodded.

"You didn't get that from killing Italians, did you?" There was a nearly imperceptible smirk on the face now.

Jim shook his head slowly. "Germans." Jim wasn't about to mention the Italians he'd killed in Sicily.

"*Bene*. Fuckin' Nazis." Badalamente took a sip of his espresso. "If anyone messes with you, Jim. Just let me know. You did stuff for this country a lot of us didn't and I don't want no one picking on you." Badalamente looked out the window. "You know what I do at Hosty. Don't be shy if I can help you." The man got up and rejoined the man he'd been sitting with, who was staring at Jim. It was Badalamente's older brother Carlo. Carlo nodded to Jim, then took a bite out of a po-boy.

Jim slowly poured two spoons of sugar in his espresso, then broke the hard pane in half. He turned to the window, his mind digesting what had just happened.

Everyone knew Hotsy Jazz was a mob club, as were many along Bourbon Street. Sal Cardone owned and ran the place and the Badalamentes worked for him. Sal was the son of Silvestri 'Silver Dollar Sam' Cardona, the boss of the New Orleans Mafia, whom Jim had never seen but heard he was a tall man with silver hair, elderly and frail.

Fat Sal was a slob who got drunk easily. He was hard on everyone, especially the girls and bartenders. Sal didn't seem to even notice the bar-backs.

The Badalamentes were the muscle of the operation. A fool could see that. They never drank and never fooled with the girls, never fooled with any employees. Hell, they never smiled. They just took care of business and everyone knew, those were the two to avoid. They weren't bouncers, huge men with low foreheads. The bouncers worked for the Badalamentes at Hotsy Jazz and kept to themselves.

As he nibbled his pane, Jim realized there was something going on between Badalamente and Sal, something menacing. He'd planned to go in early tonight, catch Desiree's final number, and now he had something to discuss with Leo Nicolosi, the head bartender. Leo had explained it to Jim right away, about the mob at the Hotsy. Leo was not Sicilian, but a Napolitano, and had no connection with the mob. He was just good at what he did and suggested Jim do the same. The Sicilians honored loyalty and were intelligent enough to recognize good workers and use them.

Jim rolled his foot around and noticed most of the pain gone now. He'd limbered it up enough and today didn't take as long as usual. A good sign. When Maria stepped back, Jim ordered his favorite dish, tortellini and took his time eating it, savoring the spicy tomato gravy, and the filing in the tortellini – cheese and beef.

The Badalamentes left without further word and Jim couldn't stop his mind from working on it. He believed in fate, luck, whatever you call it. It's what saved him in the Hürtgen and at the Battle of the Bulge, because it sure wasn't skill. When the man next to you got a bullet through the helmet from a sniper and you didn't, well that took no skill.

And now, on the Fourth of July, he runs into Desiree and then Alphonso Badalamente in two successive cafes. What were the mathematical probabilities? It had to be luck and for some strange reason, Jim thought it was running his way.

He felt a connection between him and Desiree. It might not be much, but there was something, something he could dream about at least. Jim Munster, formerly of the U.S. First Infantry Division, the Big Red One, knew dreams didn't last.

But you never knew.

He opened the paper to the amusements and went through the new features at the theaters. There was a Roy Rogers and Dale Evans flick called *Apache Rose* at the Clabon Theater, *Buffalo Bill Rides Again* with Richard Arlen and Jennifer Holt at the Carver. *Carnival in Costa Rica* starring Dick Haymes, Vera-Allen, Cesar Romero and Celeste Holm was playing at the Cortez. The theatre closest to his house, The Famous, up at North Claiborne and Marigny was showing *Angel and the Badman* with John Wayne, sultry brunette Gail Russell and Harry Carey, who usually added a little humor to a movie.

Carnival in Costa Rica? They had to be kidding?

If he was bound to see a western, John Wayne was his best bet. Jim checked the movie times and closed up his paper. He sipped his second espresso and looked out at the avenue. Across the wide neutral ground he saw people strolling through Washington Square. For a minute, he let himself imagine walking with Desiree through the square.

When the minute passed, Jim chuckled to himself. He was acting like a schoolboy. It was OK to fantasize, but if anyone was centered in reality, it was James Sean Munster. He was more likely to come across a leprechaun on the way to the streetcar as to go out on a date with Miss Desiree Blanc.

He left a nice tip, paid Mama Tantillo, tucked the newspaper under his arm and went back out into the heat. He headed for the streetcar line. He had more than enough time to catch the eight o'clock showing of *Angel and the Badman*.

Desiree's image popped into his mind again and he let it stay awhile. No harm in daydreaming, so long as he reminded himself, he was more likely to meet a girl in his league at the library, or in a bookstore, or even a restaurant, than a strip club, even if he worked the joint.

Chapter 3
LOOK WHAT HAPPENED TO BONNIE AND CLYDE

Desiree leaned close to the large mirror and spread scarlet lipstick over the pink undercoat, then she brought out a tube of bright crimson and contoured her lips. At least it wasn't a steam bath in the dressing room anymore since Fat Sal put in the new air-refrigeration system, which seemed to pull in nearly as many customers into the club as the dancers. She glanced at the wall clock in the mirror. She had ten minutes before her last performance.

"I still think this costume is cute," said Emma Rouge, who would go on after Desiree tonight.

"I'm beginning to like it too." Desiree admitted. When she'd first seen the Fourth of July costume, she'd shaken her head. A blue vest with white stars and a red and white striped skirt worn over blue panties with white stars and red pasties to cover their nipples seemed silly until the girls put the costume on. Desiree's fit very well.

From the corner of her eye, Desiree watched Emma re-apply bright red lipstick to her thin lips. Emma was the youngest girl at Hotsy, barely eighteen. A natural brunette, she'd dyed her hair red, to go along with her stage name. She was a much better dancer than Desiree and really got a kick getting the men worked up during her routine.

"Did I tell you I caught The Cat Girl's act last night?" Emma smacked her lips. "Over at the Sho Bar?"

"No."

"She gets down on all fours and purrs like a kitten, then snarls like a leopard. Wears a leopard-skin costume. She sizzles."

Desiree re-applied a light dusting of baby blue to her eye-lids. "Not like The Oyster Girl?"

"Right." Emma's brown eyes went wide. "All that slithering on stage was slimy. Especially oiled up like that." Emma had checked out Rita, The Oyster Girl over at the 500 Club and didn't like the act. Now she'd hung out at the Sho Bar to check out the competition. The Sho Bar, the 500 Club and Casino Royale were the big three clubs on Bourbon. Hotsy Jazz was too small a place to compete with the big clubs. All four clubs were owned by the Cardone family, Hotsy, Sho Bar and 500 Club outwardly. Casino Royale was run by two Jewish men who put up a good front for the Cardones, at least that's what Leo Nicolosi told Desiree in confidence.

"Here comes the roach," Emma warned as Toni Two-Lane came huffing into the dressing room, muttering to herself, dragging the remains of her costume. No way the famous Toni Two-Lane would wear a Fourth of July costume. She had her own elaborate get-ups, huge things, looking like Mardi Gras floats with feather boas, plumes and sequins.

"This goddamn place," Toni snarled. "No 'preciation for talent. All they want is skin." Toni acted as if she were the big draw at Hotsy and none of the girls argued. Toni went way back with the Cardones. She had been one of Silver Dollar Sam's mistresses when she was young.

Toni had to be in her late-forties, although insisted she was in her thirties. A full-figured gal, she wasn't a stripper, according to her. She was a burlesque dancer, one with the ability to twirl her enormous tits in opposite directions simultaneously. Her pasties looked like spinning pin wheels, which proved Desiree's conviction that men were hypnotized by tits, the bigger the better. Shiny objects on tits were even more hypnotic. Toni plopped her amble butt on the next stool just as Desiree put the finishing touches to her bright crimson lipstick.

"Break a leg," Emma said as Desiree got up.

"Shuddup!" Toni snapped. "You think this is show business?"

No use answering. Desiree winked at Emma and stepped into the dark hall to await her introduction from the emcee. She stood just inside the curtain and closed her eyes and waited.

Gun-moll – she ran it through her mind one more time to get herself up for her last performance tonight. When she'd awakened that afternoon to the stifling heat, she remained in bed for long minutes thinking she was really a gun-moll now. She had twenty-six hundred and twenty-six bucks to prove it. She planned to slip the money into the safety deposit box she'd rented at the Whitney as soon as possible.

Desiree listened to the emcee. Tonight it was Louie-Louie, one of Badalamente's boys. He wasn't bad, sounded more like he was from the Bronx than New Orleans. Desiree was still amazed how many people in New Orleans sounded like they were from New York.

"She's white hot." Louie-Louie's voice echoed over the PA system. "From the backwoods of Mississippi, she's our own white magnolia with the creamiest skin you'll ever see, white silk. She's our own white desire. Ladies and gents, we are proud to present ... Desiree Blanc."

She hoped they put the correct record on. Desiree had two acts, the first went to a new song, a rolling jazz number called "Good Rockin Tonight" by New Orleans' own Roy Brown. A boggie piano got the song moving and Desiree worked hard to put in the moves to keep up with it, but it seemed to work.

Her second act, the longer one, the one she'd end the night with was a slow, sultry strip to another new song but another New Orleanian, Charley Graham. "Lonesome Little Blue" started with a saxophone rift and slid through a deceptive drum beat that she matched beat-for-beat with the slow movement of her hips.

The first strains of the sax drew her through the red curtain into the dark club filled with cigar and cigarette smoke. Concentrating on the music, Desiree matched the drumbeat, swaying her hips, as she continued down the dance floor. The place was packed for a Friday night. Holiday traffic, white faces leering out of the smoke like ghosts, most smiling, some gaping, eyes boring into her, watching, examining her as if she were under a microscope. It was better to think of them as anonymous, although some of the faces were familiar.

When she reached the end of the stage, she planted her feet apart and lifted her skirt and someone howled. Turning her butt to them, she rolled it, closing her feet and working her panties down, keeping her legs locked, raising her ass high until she stepped out of the panties and kicked them back up the stage.

Desiree continued moving slowly, sensuously as the top came off, then the skirt, until she had only the spiked high heels, pasties and white g-string. The song shifted gears, the beat rising slightly and she floated with it from the front of the stage to the rear, up and down each side. When the song ended, another record came right on, this one also bluesy and she continued her routine, bending over, then going down on all fours. She rolled on her back and raised her feet straight up, opening them slowly until she lay spread-eagle on the stage.

She caressed her breasts and there were the usual calls of, "I can help you with that."

She gyrated her hips, lifting her ass from the floor. She rolled over and did a spider crawl to change positions to give the men on one side a view of her crotch, did it again to give the other side a view before getting up slowly as the original song started again and she was at the half-way point of her routine. Desiree worked the sides of the stage, looking at the faces now, recognizing regulars, spotting the Badalamentes. Facing the bar she spotted Leo and saw the bar-back, Jim Munster. She gave him a wink and continued on. She didn't see Bogarde, but he usually sat at the front of the club near the door.

Desiree knew the strength of her act wasn't dancing, which was why she moved slowly, and it wasn't even her tits, although Bogarde swore it was her tits. She knew it was the aloof way she pranced, the way she paid little or no attention to the audience. It was as if they were peeking at a private ritual where a long, tall white-ash blond let them peek at her taking off her clothes. It tapped man's voyeuristic nature, which none of the other girls did. They played to the crowd, some even talking with the men.

Desiree was beyond their touch, beyond them completely, but nice enough to let them see her body. She got down to g-string and pasties early and remained as naked as the legal limit for as long as she was on stage, then she pranced off and didn't go out, like many of the other girls, to mingle with the crowd.

Mingling was a problem at Hotsy Jazz. Fat Sal wanted his girls to become B-girls, coaxing drinks from the marks. The drinks were, of course, tea, while the marks were charged for the real stuff. Only the Badalamentes wouldn't allow B-drinking in Hotsy, although the Cardone family did with the big clubs, the Sho Bar and Casino Royale. The vice squad was paid to look the other way. Desiree learned, again from Leo the bartender, that B-drinking made everyone unhappy – the marks, the girls and the bartenders.

Entering the dressing room she found Alphonso Badalamente sitting at the dressing table. Dressed in all black, he dabbed his moustache and said, "I've got a request for you."

Desiree popped off the pasties and put on her brassiere. Since Badalamente had taken over the girls at Hotsy, the pressure was off for them to B-drink and turn tricks away from the club. Not that Desiree had done either, but Fat Sal used to proposition them for customers. For a moment Desiree wondered if something had changed. Badalamente said, "A regular. Harmless man actually. I checked him out. Wants you to pose for him. Pictures. Nudes, of course." He got up, leaving a business card on the table. "He says he'll pay top dollar and I can send an escort."

He walked out without waiting for an answer, adding, "Let me know what you wanna do."

Desiree picked up the card. It read: Dennis Schroeder Photography. There was a Royal Street address and a phone number.

Two of the girl who went on after midnight hustled in giggling. Desiree heard Emma's music rise as her act began. Desiree dressed quickly and got out before the other two girls from midnights arrived. She barely knew them and they didn't seem particularly friendly.

In a sleeveless white blouse and black Capri pants, low heels, Desiree carried her purse and travel bag into the club and headed straight for the bar for an icy club soda. Leo had it ready for her as she sat between two men in suits. Both gave her a look but neither seemed to realize who she was. She was the only ash blond in the entire joint but most of the men didn't see anything above her neck when she was on stage. If she didn't see it for herself, she wouldn't believe it.

Leo leaned over and said, "Good work tonight."

She gave him a warm smile. Leo Nicolosi was the senior bartender, a thick man with large arms, tattoos running down both, a large USMC on one arm, an Eiffel tower on the other. She'd learned a little about him a few weeks back when she came in early, a slow day, so she sat at the bar and talked with him. He was sixty, a veteran of the First World War and wasn't one of Badalamente's boys. It was Leo who'd confirmed Cardone and

Badalamente were mobbed-up, saying back then he couldn't be one of them because he wasn't Sicilian.

She took a sip of icy-cold club soda. She spotted Jim's face behind Leo and winked at him again. He nodded a smile and began filling one of the coolers with bottles of Schlitz, the beer that made Milwaukee famous. Desiree turned to watch Emma for a minute. The young gal was enthusiastic, bouncing as she danced. She had the crowd going, some of the men actually clapping to the driving beat of the boogie-woogie song she stripped to.

Desiree felt a hand on her shoulder and turned to Bogarde's face. He leaned close and said, "Ready?"

She thanked Leo with a nod and followed Bogarde out. Would have been nice if he'd carried one of her bags. He stopped just inside the doorway, looked to his right and waited for her. When she got close, he leaned against her ear.

"See the stiff in the green suit?"

It took a moment to spot a balding, roly-poly man sipping a high ball as he stared at Emma.

"That's our next mark," Bogarde added and led her out.

It was still muggy outside even after midnight, the air thick and hot. It didn't cool down after dark, it just got dark. The banquette was crowded and they had to worm their way through.

"Our next mark?" Desiree switched her clothes bag from one shoulder to the other.

"He's a freakin' banker. Chartres National Bank on Carondelet Street. His wife doesn't know, but he's a stripper-freak.

"You want to rob a bank?"

"Sort of." Bogarde was being cute, flashing her that smile, bouncing as he walked. Tonight he was in another pair of cream-colored pants and a dark blue shirt, black and white wing tips. He sure liked cream-colored pants.

"Sort of? Look what happened to Bonnie and Clyde."

Bogarde got a good laugh out of that but Desiree wasn't joking. She had to call out, "Hey," to get him to slow down and when he turned back to her, she shoved the travel bag at him. "Once in a while you can act like a gentleman."

He took the bag with a huff and led on.

"Where are we going?" she asked.

"To eat."

That, she knew. She always ate after getting off, her only real meal of the day. She'd had coffee and a roll for breakfast and nibbled Ritz crackers before going to work. They went all the way to Dumaine Street where they cut across to the Clover Grill. At least Bogarde opened the door for her and she stepped into the wonderful smell of burgers cooking on a grill. There was only one table open and they worked their way pass the crowded counter where a couple men gave Desiree the eye as she passed.

It was a table for two and Bogarde put his back to the door. Desiree settled in and picked up a menu. Voices in the small place echoed off the windows facing Bourbon Street. There were no strip joints along this part of Bourbon, no nightclub, no shops. It was mostly residential here, except for the occasional café and this grill.

"I'm having the usual," said Bogarde. Desiree sighed and said, "Me too. But have them cut mine in half."

Bogarde was too impatient to wait for the waitress so he went back up to the cash register and ordered, bringing their drinks back with them, Coca-Cola for him, Barq's root beer for her. He leaned over and said, "I'll lay it out for you."

She took a sip of icy Barq's.

"His name's James Gallagher. Manages the Chartres National Bank. Wife's a librarian. They got two kids."

Desiree watched the grill man work the burgers. He wore a thick oven mitt on his left hand which he used to lift the hub caps from atop the burgers and used a spatula to flip them. The hub caps were purchased new and were the most fancy available, some Rolls Royce, Cadillac, Jaguar.

"See that moustache he wore tonight?"

"Moustache?"

Bogarde's eyes bulged. "Gallagher. In the club. The moustache he wore is fake."

"Oh." The man had a moustache?

Someone belched loudly at the counter.

"This could be a big score," Bogarde added. "A bank."

"I still don't get it. Robbing a bank?"

"More like stealing from a bank. No guns at all. Well, maybe we'll show a gun." He leaned close again and said, "Soon as the grub gets here, I'll lay it out to you."

Desiree looked out at the dark night. Across the street were typical French Quarter buildings of wood with black lace-work balconies. All were dark, the occupants probably sleeping. Cars zipped down Bourbon Street, their headlights dancing on the wooden buildings. The balconies were Spanish, as was most of the architecture here. Someone had told her that when she arrived. Apparently most of the original French buildings had burned and the city rebuilt during Spanish rule. Something like that. Oh yeah, and one of the buildings, maybe the only one to survive both times the Quarter burned was the Ursuline Convent. A miracle.

The same nuns, along with the entire Catholic clergy had prayed fanatically to the city's patron saint, Our Lady of Prompt Succor, to deliver them from the bloody British at the Battle of New Orleans. The Americans won a miraculous victory. Prompt Succor. Funny name.

The burgers were brought by one of the two waitresses, a skinny woman who had to be pushing fifty. Desiree's burger was cut in half. She peeked at it and it was well done, the way she liked it. Bogarde's oozed blood. He snatched his up and took a huge bite and spoke with his mouth full.

"You need to … get chummy … with the mark."

"How chummy?"

Bogarde had to wait to swallow some of his food. Desiree took a bite of her burger. Hot, delicious and very spicy. Best burger in town.

"You know," Bogarde finally said. "Flirt. Kissy-face. Maybe a little touchy-feely. Get him dreaming."

"So that's it? I kiss him. Let him paw me and he gives us a lotta money."

"Don't be cute. You get him hooked on Desiree. We visit him at the bank. Ask him to show us the vault. Show him the gun and fill up two bags fulla cash and walk out." Bogarde tried his eyes on her. "We tell him he can't hit the alarm for ten minutes. We're long gone by the time the cops come."

"And he just gives them our descriptions."

"I'll be wearing a disguise and he won't tell them who you are because we'll tell his wife on him."

Desiree took another bite of burger, then a fry, then a sip of Barq's before she said, "The other people in the bank will describe me."

"Women mostly. They won't recognize you. They don't go to strip clubs."

They each took another bite. Desiree thinking about this, asking, "Who are you supposed to be when we go into the bank together?"

"Your brother."

She almost choked. "I talk southern and you don't. We grew up in different houses?"

"I'll think of something. Just leave it to me."

Desiree took another bite and looked at the darkness outside again. They ate the rest of their meal in silence, Desiree stuffing half her burger in a bag to take home. Bogarde paid the bill but she made sure to leave the tip so the waitress would get something.

On their way out, Desiree said, "When we go to the bank, you could be my investment lawyer."

"They have investment lawyers?" Bogarde cracked.

"Sure. You're one."

• • •

Jim Munster watched Desiree leave with her boyfriend, shrugged to himself and finished loading up the cooler. He'd seen the stiff come in, cigarette dangling from his lips, hair curled as if he'd just come from a beauty salon, looking a little like Errol Flynn. The man sat at the bar and sipped a fuzzy navel (orange juice, vodka and peach liquor), a chick drink. The man seemed to pay more attention to the customers than Desiree when she came out for her act. Then again, he'd seen it, touched it, maybe was bored with it. Jim watched Desiree as much as he could as he worked.

The crowd cheered loudly, bringing Jim back to the present. He watched Emma as she pulled her g-string down a little to show some of her bush, then pulled it back up quickly, turned and rolled her butt as she pranced to the music. She ended her act with a bow to the audience, her ass up in the air facing them. Sometimes the girl could sizzle.

The senior bartender, Leo Nicolosi, tapped the biggest sink on his way to snatch a bottle of Crown Royal from in front of the bar mirror. Jim moved straight to the sink and began washing the glasses. Emma's music ended and the drone of talk rose again. Jim let himself think of Desiree, how different she looked in a blouse and slacks, still pretty as hell. And how different she looked last night in that red dress.

Since Desiree and Jim had the same days off, this was their first shift back this week. The workers at Hotsy Jazz worked six days on and two off, their off-days rotating every week so eventually everyone got a weekend off. There were two bar-backs working each shift, except tonight because the new guy had called in sick. Jim didn't mind the hard work, only it took away from learning to tend bar. There was a relief bartender, a quiet guy named Ralph who worked the far end of the bar where the waitresses picked up their drinks. Jim never knew any of the waitress' names as they came and went almost weekly, it seemed.

Leo, the old WWI vet, had taken Jim under his wing and gave him free bartender lessons. Jim was a fast learner and really applied himself to the task, learning the differences between sour mash and malt liquors, the incredible number of scotches, bourbons and vodkas, not to mention the gins and rums. He'd been memorizing the mixture of the high-balls, the easy to mix rum-and-Coke, then the manhattans and martinis, long island iced-tea, screwdrivers, slow gin fizz, Cuba Libre, Harvey Wallbanger, a multitude of daiquiris, the incredibly sweet banana banshee, it went on and on.

Lately, Leo had started in on the beers, the different types of ales, lagers, pilsner and bitters as well as the regular American beers and some light beer from Belgium called Stella Artois. There was Moosehead from Canada, Loggerhead from Iceland, Beck's from West Germany, Heineken from Holland, Foster's from Australia and a host of English beers. The had all of the American standards – Falstaff, Schlitz, Budweiser, Miller High Life, Carling, Pabst Blue Ribbon, and the local beers, Dixie and Jax, and a lot more.

"So, what'd you see tonight?" asked Leo.

"*Angel and the Badman*. John Wayne and Gail Russell."

Leo popped a Carling and handed it to a customer. "I like his westerns better n' his war movies, since I was in the Great War. Maybe you too?"

"Some of the war flicks were good." Jim wiped down the counter with a damp rag. "Especially 'They Were …'."

"Expendable," Leo cut him off. "Yeah. That's a good one." Leo went down the bar to serve an impatient customer waving at him. Jim grabbed the broom and swept up behind the bar.

Jim saw the fight develop from the start. A new stripper was up on stage, one of the midnight girls, one of the dyed-blonds, and a drunk tried to grab her leg as she passed. Another drunk took offense and slammed a fist against the side of the first drunk's head only the first drunk was a big man, a very big man, a damn big man who stood up, grabbed the second drunk by the front of the man's shirt and tossed him over two tables. This offended the patrons at both tables as their drinks went sailing.

The melee lasted until Badalamente's two bouncers made it from the front of Hotsy and began tossing the participants out on Bourbon Street. They reached the damn big man last and he tried to fight them. Baddie's bouncers weren't as tall but they were broader and had previously broken noses and scarred hands (Jim had seen their hands up close and they looked like gnarled catcher's mitts). The drunk tried to punch one and both hit him, one in the stomach, the other in the jaw and the man went down liked a felled tree. As they dragged him out, Jim saw the bouncers smile. They rarely smiled. They dragged the damn big drunk to the sidewalk and left him there.

Leo stood next to Jim, hand up on Jim's shoulder, and said, "That's how it's done, young man. Short and sweet."

Later, during the usual four a.m. lull, Leo explained a little about the bouncers. "Joe and Joe-Joe are what we call button men. Alphonso Badalamente, who's a capo or captain, has them push a button and they do. Strong-arm stuff, protection stuff and worse."

"Seriously?" Jim sipped the extra strong coffee-and-chicory Leo made at four a.m. No cream, just plenty of sugar. They were at the far end of the bar, between sets. Ralph, the relief bartender worked the few customers at the bar. Leo was giving Jim another lesson about the mob.

"La Cosa Nostra, as Lucky Luciano calls it, means 'our thing' or 'this thing of ours'. It's the American Mafia, centered in New York City with five families, as I told you before." Leo's dark brown eyes danced as he took a hit of his coffee. "The family here used to be called the Giacona Family until Corrado 'Big C' died in '44. That's when Silvestri took over. You ever see him?"

"Nope."

"Silvestri 'Silver Dollar Sam' Cardone became the don and his son, our wonderful, cheerful, slob of an owner, 'Fat Sal' Cardone is the family's underboss. Second in command. They have several Capos, besides Alphonso Badalamente. I showed you 'Joe Pig' and 'Tony the Ant'. They come in once in a while."

"What about Carlo?" Alphonso's brother Carlo was the quietest man Jim had ever seen. The man rarely talked and stared right through you with those beady, black-brown eyes.

"Button man or soldati, soldier. He's not as clever as his younger brother." Leo leaned closer. "I heard he's the most efficient eliminator."

Jim almost smiled. If it all wasn't true, it would sound like a bad 'B' movie. "But you're not mobbed up."

"How many times I gotta tell 'ya. I'm Napolitano. These guys are Sicilian. I could button for them but never be a made man so what's the point? You, on the other hand, being a pure Irish Mick, you could take out the garbage but that's about it."

"By take out the garbage, you mean do some unpleasant things but never meet the big shots?"

"No, I mean empty their garbage cans, maybe wash the toilets. They got no use for us, except what we do there at Hotsy. We work. We see nothing and we say nothing to anyone except maybe to each other. Capiche?"

Jim took another hit of coffee, looked around the place. He was caught up with his bar-backing for the evening and found this was an unusually quiet Friday night. Maybe the end of a long Fourth of July day. On weekdays, the four a.m. lull was pretty dead but weekends popped, except tonight.

"Think the fight cleaned out the place?"

"They got some new gals on midnights over at Casino Royale. The family owns that one too."

Jim heard that.

Leo smirked. "The girl's over there will get totally naked tonight. Special show."

Jim had to ask, "How you know all this stuff?"

"I listen."

"What about this guy who goes out with Desiree?"

"The pretty boy? Thinks he's God's gift to women?"

"Yeah. He mobbed up?"

Leo coughed up the coffee he was swallowing, wiped up the counter with a rag as he coughed. Jim patted him on the back.

Leo finally caught his breath. "He looks like a *finochio* to me. A fruit. He's not even Italian so he can never be mobbed up."

Jim finished his coffee and asked if Leo wanted a re-fill. He re-filled both cups and stepped back.

Leo looked him in the eye. "She's different than the other gals, all right. Genuine beauty and she ain't been here long enough to be ruined. But don't go fallin' for her. She's got a whole different take on life, my young friend."

"Whaddya mean?"

"She's in it for the money."

Jim's brow furrowed. "How do …"

"Just watch and listen and you'll learn everything you need to survive. How I got to be sixty."

Alphonso Badalamente and his brother came out of the back room and went through the club. Usually they didn't look around, but Badalamente glanced their way and subtly nodded to Jim on their way out.

Leo said, "What was that?"

"I ran into him this afternoon at a café."

"You don't run into him. He runs into you. Tell me what happened." Leo leaned close and Jim told him the whole conversation.

"Curious," Leo said. "But it ain't bad."

"How do you know?"

"If it was bad. You wouldn't hear anything. These guys play for keeps."

When Jim's relief was late for work, he told Fat Sal he could stay on.

"Naw. Get outta here. We got someone comin'. You think of maybe getting overtime or somethin'? Just cause you're a vet?" Well, well. Fat Sal did know who he was after all.

Jim was happy to get away from Fat Sal's cigar. Leo had already left so Jim stepped out and walked down Bourbon, walking in the street to avoid the bouncers hosing down the sidewalks outside the clubs. Damn, it stank of stale beer, vomit, piss and rotting garbage. This part of Bourbon always stank so Jim took the first side street and walked down to Chartres.

He didn't feel like going up to take a streetcar so he walked through the Quarter. Away from Bourbon Street the Quarter didn't smell as bad, but still had that old smell to it. Old timbers, musty, the occasional scent of drying paint as someone spruced up one of the Creole cottages or re-painted a wooden building. Good smells too wafted across Jim, food cooking, garlic and the sweet scents of meat sizzling, bacon or sausages.

The clock atop St. Louis Cathedral said it was eight fifteen as Jim passed Jackson Square. A couple artists were setting up their wares along the black, wrought iron fence surrounding the square. Jim saw the masts of a passing ship beyond the sea wall and smelled the river now, the deep muddy smell.

Later, as he closed in on Esplanade Avenue, came the smells from the French market, bananas, bell peppers, garlic again. It was busier along the lower end of the Quarter. Mostly residential, this area was more run-down with bigger families crowded into the small places. He crossed Esplanade to head into the Faubourg Marigny when a flash of ash-blond hair caught his attention. Jim stopped in the center of Esplanade and watched Desiree Blanc approach.

She wore a sleeveless baby blue blouse and white Capri pants, white pumps and had only a breath of make-up on. She spotted him, her jaw dropping for a second before she composed herself and came straight to him.

"Just got up," she said, brushing a strand of hair from her eyes. "Join me for a cup of java?"

Jim nodded. She took his hand and led him to the sidewalk as a gray DeSoto approached, driven by the same dark-haired man, sure looked like a detective.

"Just got off, huh?" she said, letting go of his hand and leading the way down Esplanade toward the French Market. "Morning Call OK with you?"

"Sure."

Morning Call never closed. Coffee and French pastries called beignets, donuts without holes covered in powdered sugar, was the specialty but they could have served rotten meat for all Jim cared. He felt his heart racing as they walked, caught a whiff of her light perfume and had to wonder.

Did I just run into her or did she run into me?

Chapter 4
YOU STIR THE SOULS OF MEN AND BEASTS

Jim took a bite of beignet, careful not to blow off any of the powdered sugar. The pastry was almost too hot to eat, fresh out of the deep fryer. They sat next to each other on wooden seats at the marble counter in the center of the Morning Call Coffee Stand while waiters in all white, including hats, moved in and out with trays full of coffee and beignets to the cars parked along Decatur Street. Fans suspended from the high ceiling kept the place comfortable.

"They smell delicious," Desiree said as she raised her cup of strong café-au-lait. She had to put sugar in it, but eating powdered sugar-covered-donuts wasn't what her figure needed. Men were lucky, could eat anything. This stuff was Toni Two-Lane fare.

Jim took a sip of his coffee, which he took black but needed three sugars, then told her *Angel and the Bad Man* wasn't a bad flick.

"You go to movies every day?"

"Just about."

Jim watched Desiree's eyes as they spoke. Maybe it was the light, but they seemed to shine even brighter and seemed an even lighter shade of blue. Above the counter, running beneath a wooden archway with the café's name on it, was a line of incandescent light bulbs, which, added to the walls of windows on every side of the café and the white marble floor, made the place very bright.

"So what's at the show tonight?"

"Haven't looked at the paper yet, but there's a double feature at the Circle, down at St. Bernard and Galvez. *King Kong* and *Island of Lost Souls* with Charles Laughton and the Panther woman who lures men … only to destroy them, body and soul. There were two exclamation points after the word 'soul' in the ad."

Desiree was grinning broadly now. "There's a cat girl over at the Sho Bar.

"Well, this one was once a real panther and the evil scientist turned her into a human."

"I think most of our customers were gorillas before a mad scientist turned them human. Ever go to the zoo?"

"The one in Oklahoma City."

"The one here, the Audubon Zoo, has these two gorillas and I swear, they stare at me with the same look in their eyes the customers have. The chimps have that look too."

Jim grinned, "You stir the souls of men and beasts."

Desiree almost coughed up her coffee again in front of Jim. Men and beasts? She wondered what he'd think if she told him she was the beauty in the 'beauty-and-the-beast gang'. She glanced at the electric clock on the wall and it was only a little after nine.

"I'm waiting until the shops on Canal open at ten," she said. "Maybe we should take in a movie together, sometime."

It was Jim's turn to almost cough up his coffee.

The man sitting across the counter got off his stool and said, "Don't mean to interrupt, but I caught your act over at Hotsy and think you're too good for that place." He was young, in his twenties, tall, broad shoulders with slick-black hair. "No, I'm not one of the lurkers. I play tenor sax over at the 500 Club. Louis Prima's band. You two kids have a nice day." And he walked out.

Desiree and Jim both took sips of coffee. The man had acted as if they were a couple and for a moment it was as if the air had been sucked out of the room for Jim. When he glanced at Desiree, she shrugged her shoulders.

Desiree was thinking they probably looked and acted like a couple with all the eye contact. She wondered if she and Bogarde looked like a *couple*. Then she thought how the big clubs, like the 500 Club, had live bands, instead of records and wondered what it would be like to strip in front of a hundred people, instead of dozens. Couples went to the big clubs, husband and wives, men with their mistresses. Few women not in the business went into Hotsy Jazz.

"I've heard Fat Sal talk about Louis Prima," she said. "He gripes how the big clubs draw them in with bands, comedians and bigger stripper acts."

Jim stared into his coffee. "I think Louis Prima did 'Way Down Yonder in New Orleans' and 'I'm Just a Gigolo' the 'I Ain't Got Nobody' song. Fat Sal loves the guy. Leo says Badalamente has another take, criticizing Prima with all his monkey-shines on stage, mugging for the crowds and unflattering songs about Italians like, 'Don't Squeeza Da Banana' and 'Josephina, Please No Leana on the Bell'."

"You sure know a lot."

"I keep quiet, watch and listen."

That drew a big smile from her as she finished her coffee. She put her right elbow up on the counter, her chin cupped in open palm of her hand and looked into his eyes. "So what do you think of my act?"

"It's nice. Slow and nice." His eye-brows rose.

She gave him another big smile. "I'll bet you say that to all the girls."

"They don't have your style."

"I have style?"

"The slow way you move. It's seductive as hell."

"Glad you approve." Her voice had a teasing, smart-aleck lilt to it as she snatched up her purse. "I have to go now and you need some sleep." She squeezed his shoulder as she climbed off her stool. "Let me know about the panther girl."

As she walked out, he said, "Panther woman."

"Right." She waved over her shoulder and stepped into the early morning heat. A couple of the cars had their engines running. Air-conditioned, no doubt. Someone tapped his horn as she passed and Desiree thought – gorilla. Tapping a horn, howling from construction sites, wolf whistling, that's as far as men had evolved in trying to attract the fairer sex.

She went over to Royal Street to look in the antique shops as she moved up to Canal. There was a lot of old fashioned furniture, lamps, vases and jewelry in the window displays. As she crossed Bienville Street, a large Negro, hosing down the street, turned the hose away and she tip-toed over the wet pavement. He looked her in the eye when she passed and didn't look away as she looked back.

"Good morning," she said, figuring she'd surprise him.

"Good morning yourself, ma'am." He gave her a smile and she moved on. At least he didn't look down and mumble.

The first time Desiree saw a Negro was when she was thirteen, on a trip to Tupelo and she tried not to stare at the dark skin. She thought their skin looked velvety and couldn't figure why her relatives disliked them so much, always said bad things about them. There were no Negro families around Wolf's Bark, Mississippi. There were sure plenty in New Orleans.

None were allowed in Hotsy Jazz of course, but she flashed one a few weeks ago. She'd just got to work and stepped into the courtyard behind Hotsy after putting on her make-up for a breath of air as the air-conditioning wasn't working too well that day and the place was too smoky. She had on her g-string and high heels. The man was working on a brick wall at the rear of the patio area and was half-hidden by a tree. She didn't see him at first, but when he moved from behind a tree, she noticed him but pretended she didn't see him.

She raised her arms and put her hands behind her head and closed her eyes. She felt the man's eyes on her. It was completely different, standing in the evening sunlight, outside, in only a g-string with a man who wasn't supposed to see her, a man staring at her. She could imagine his heart racing as hers raced.

She opened her eyes and he was just staring at her. She giggled and put her hands on her hips. He took the baseball cap from his head and held it up. He was about twenty yards away, a middle-aged man with skin the color of tree bark and a bright smile on his face.

"Didn't mean to startle you," she said. Turning, Desiree wiggled her ass at him as she went back into Hotsy. She was so juiced up, she had a hard time keeping still. It stayed with her through her shift. She kept wondering what he thought, wondering if he'd been daydreaming about the naked white woman. As soon as she got off that night, she took Bogarde's hand and almost dragged him to his apartment where she attacked him right on his sofa to relieve the frustration. Coming up for air after, Bogarde asked what had gotten into her. Then he noticed she'd put a wrinkle in his new slacks. Sometimes, he was such a chimp.

She spied a pay phone on the corner of Royal and Iberville and pulled the card Alphonso Badalamente left her. She noticed the

Royal Street address and realized she probably just walked past the place. She dropped a nickel in the phone and dialed the number.

A man's deep voice answered and she asked, "Is this Dennis Schroeder Photography?"

"Yes. I'm Dennis Schroeder." The voice quickened a little.

"Mister Badalamente gave me your card. This is Desiree Blanc."

"Oh my, Miss Blanc. I'm so glad you called." The voice definitely quickened. "I've seen your act and would like to photograph you. As a model."

No kiddin'.

"What kind of pictures are we talking about, Mr. Schroeder?" A black car trailing smoke drove by and Desiree waved the fumes away with her clutch purse.

"Call me Dennis. I'd like to take some nudes, some artistic nudes," the voice deepened, getting serious now. "I have a patio behind my studio and there's a wonderful afternoon light. Nothing like natural light and I'm sure your fair complexion will stand out in stark contrast to the dark walls surrounding my patio. It's quite private actually."

"How much do you pay?"

"For Desiree Blanc, two hundred dollars for two hours work."

She let him wait a few second before she said, "I'll have someone with me, since you're a stranger."

"Certainly. Senore Badalamente made that clear and that's fine. So you'll do it?"

"Well," she let a few seconds go by, thinking she'd like to get some good nudes done of her. "Will I get copies of the pictures?"

"Absolutely."

"OK, when?"

"Senore Badalamente says you work four to midnight, so any afternoon around one p.m. would work fine."

"I'll check my social calendar and call you back."

"May I have a number to contact you?"

"Try Hotsy Jazz. Bye. Bye." And she hung up.

Desiree reached Canal Street and stood on the corner. It was Saturday on main street with streetcars lumbering down the neutral ground and shoppers already moving in and out of the big stores –

D. H. Holmes, Maison Blanche, Godchaux's, Rubenstein Brothers, Depardieu's. She tucked her purse under her left arm and headed for D. H. Holmes Department Store where the discriminating woman shopped for clothes, shoes, perfume and jewelry. She had two hundred of Elmer's money in her purse and planned to spend all of it. Hell, she'd earn it back posing for Schroeder and it was *Saturday* on Canal Street.

• • •

On Sunday morning, Bogarde liked to sleep late, take his time dressing, then go down to Jackson Square to troll for women. On the Sunday after the 'beauty-and-the-beast gang' scored their first success, he went out on the front stoop earlier than normal to get his morning paper. There hadn't been anything in Saturday's, July 5th paper, so if there was a police report it had to be in the big Sunday edition. Only his paper wasn't there.

"Son-of-a-bitch," he scowled as he looked around. Someone had pilfered his paper. It had happened once before but not in a while. After a minute or two, realizing he looked silly in his pajamas and went back in. He tried to just go back to sleep but that didn't work so he took a long shower, shaved and put on an aqua-colored shirt and white pants, white shoes and belt and strolled down to Jackson Square.

Passing the small A&P Food Store at the corner of Bourbon and St. Ann Streets, he went in for a Sunday paper. He bought a pink carnation from an old woman selling flowers outside The Place D'Armes Hotel. He would use the flower as a bookmark as he thumbed through the paper at Café DuMonde, the coffee-and-beignet café catty-corner from Jackson Square. He sat under the striped awning of the outdoor café and ordered café-au-lait from the waiter. He spread the newspaper out on the small round table.

He found the police reports as the coffee arrived. He dropped in a couple spoons of sugar, stirred and scanned through the list of crimes reported to police the previous week – nine burglaries, one suicide, one rape, two stabbings, two shooting where no one died, a host of thefts and four armed robberies. None of them reported out in the eastern part of the city, out by Lake Catherine where they'd left Elmer and nothing reported at the Jung Hotel. Damn. How the hell would anyone know about the 'beauty-and-the-beast gang' if chumps like Elmer didn't report it to the police? Damn, he wanted to see it in print. *Visitor jacked by 'beauty-and-the-beast gang'.*

His scanned down to the more detailed crime stories, the first entitled, 'Cardsharp Clipped'. Apparently, a Detroit man talked his way into a card game with a podiatrist he visited and fleeced the doctor, two dentist friends and a chiropodist of nearly ten grand over a three week period. The poker games were held at the house of the podiatrist the first evening and the houses of the dentists on two successive Friday night sessions. At the second to last session, the sharp-eyed chiropodist suspected the cardsharp dealing of the bottom of the deck and called his brother-in-law, a New Orleans police sergeant who joined the game last Friday evening where the cardsharp was spotted second dealing and dealing off the bottom of the deck. The sergeant described the cardsharp's 'second dealing' and 'subway dealing' off the bottom.

When nabbed, the cardsharp gave the name Joseph Smith to police, who quickly determined he had a half dozen previous aliases and nine previous arrests. The medical men were victims as Louisiana law protects private games, however, any gambling enterprise in which the house or host takes a cut, is a violation of Louisiana law. Ha! What about the casinos on Friscoville Avenue in St. Bernard Parish or The Beverly out in Jefferson Parish? And those were just the ones Bogarde heard about. There had to be more lucrative gambling establishments known only to old line native New Orleanians.

The second detailed police report was titled, 'Con-artists Collared'. A man and a woman team of con-artists, traveling grifters, mostly small time, were caught by the bunko squad after lifting two grand from two elderly men. The blond and her black haired accomplice were also suspected in a couple hold-ups. There were small pictures accompanying the story, the blond not bad looking but the man looked like an ex-prize fighter with a droopy left eye and broken nose. How he talked anyone into anything was amazing. For a moment, Bogarde thought that maybe these two would take the heat off. Maybe one of those hold-ups these two were suspected of was Elmer.

He scanned the café again, looking for another tourist to clip, like Elmer, looking for a replacement for Fanny who was getting too comfortable with him as she entered the second stage of their relationship. The first stage, when a woman did just about anything to attract Bogarde, was the best stage. In the second stage, they started expecting things, like calling him at work and wanting to know where he lived and what he was thinking after sex. Bogarde always bolted in the second stage, except with Desiree. There were no stages with her. They just fell in together, like Bonnie and Clyde.

He sipped his coffee and looked around the café. Most tourist families, snot-nosed kids wolfing down beignets. No lone woman sitting by herself. Sometimes, before or after church let out at the cathedral, a lone woman would stroll across the square for a belt of sugar.

Maybe it was too hot out. Even in the morning, he felt the humidity heavy in the air, especially near the river. As if to punctuate his thought, a boat's horn sounded on the other side of the concrete sea wall. The Mississippi was about a hundred yards beyond the wall along the back side of the café.

Two women sat at another outdoor table, both checking him out. One was too old, the other ugly. Bogarde left ten cents for the coffee and a nickel tip, crossed Decatur Street and went into Jackson Square. A huge flock of pigeons bopped on the ground in front of Bogarde and opened for him like waves on a pond. Several kids were feeding the pigeons and one emptied his paper bag, blew it up and popped it, sending the pigeons into the air.

Pigeon wings flapped against Bogarde's hair, a big one careened off his shoulder and he covered his head hoping nothing dropped on him. He made it safely to Andrew Jackson's statue, the American general rearing on a horse, both covered in pigeon shit. There were a few people sitting on the wrought iron benches arranged in a circle not far from the statue, which was in the center of the small square; but there were only couples and some old men.

Bogarde got out of there before another pigeon attack, heading for the exit next to the cathedral. It was a pretty cathedral made of stucco with three spires, European architecture definitely, gothic revival, with a modern electric clock on its face that showed it was a quarter after ten.

Crossing Chartres Street, he walked in front of the Presbytere building next to the cathedral, crossed St. Ann Street and continued down Chartres. He would have to turn left eventually to get up to Rampart Street and St. Alice's Hall, run by the Knights of Columbus, where there was always a social gathering after Sunday mass for parishioners from the various parishes in and around the French Quarter. It was prime picking ground for lonely women.

He was thinking, the 'beauty-and-the-beast' gang needed to hit the paper, needed to make a splash when he came to a small jewelry store and stopped. He slowly backed across the narrow street, leaned on a wrought iron support railing of a balcony and looked at the place. It was perfect. He could park on Chartres or better still the small street that led to Decatur, Madison Avenue, just one block long and like all French Quarter Streets with parking on one side of the street.

Roth Brothers Jewelers occupied a one-story, narrow wooden building with two picture windows and a door with an oval glass plane facing Chartres Street. There was an aisle down the center of the store with glass cases on either side and a skinny walkway behind each case. The building was actually set back a little from the other buildings which abutted the sidewalk. It gave the place a cave-like appearance and looking inside wasn't easy unless you were right in front of the place or directly across the street, as Bogarde stood.

A plan began to form in Bogarde's mind as he walked away briskly. They'd have to break up the jewelry, get the stones out to fence, not that he knew any fences, but the place had to have cash. Get Desiree to wear a slinky outfit, go in showing skin and blond hair, put her in dark sunglasses. Maybe fire a shot on the way out, telling them it was the 'beauty-and-the-beast-gang' with him wearing that gorilla mask.

He could picture the news article – Daring Daylight Robbery by the Beauty-and-the-Beast Gang. He was bound get an argument from Desiree because the smart thing was to stay *out* of the paper, but you could go to jail in this business and if he had to, he'd rather go famous, than just some punk heisting people.

Maybe he should just call the newspaper, tell them about the gang and about Elmer. Tell the reporter on the desk he was the 'beast' from the gang. He'd have to think about it. Get the words right. Maybe write them down.

He was feeling pretty good when he walked into St. Alice's Hall, ready to ask the first lonely looking woman if it was St. Alice of Wonderland or St. Alice Through the Looking Glass, when he almost bumped into Elmer, the mark from Topeka he and Desiree had left in his drawers alongside Highway 90.

• • •

"So how was the movie?" Desiree asked as she sat at the bar that night. She'd put on a sleeveless red blouse and black Capri slacks and pinned her hair up on the sides.

"Didn't go," Jim said as he washed glasses in the big stainless steel sink.

"So you didn't see the panther girl?"

He had to smile, although his foot was still killing him. That's why he'd passed on the movie and stayed home, having to take two of those pain pills just to get through the day. "Panther woman," he said.

Leo put a club soda in front of Desiree as he passed and she winked at him.

"So, you went cruising for chicks instead?" she asked Jim.

"Sure did. Found one on the street. Alley cat woman. She was purring as I approached."

Desiree took a hit of club soda and kept looking into his eyes. He almost said, "What?"

The stare continued and he was sure her eyes were telling him something. He just wasn't sure what. Then she said, "So you're from Oklahoma?"

"Huh? Uh, yeah." That's right. He'd told her he'd gone to the zoo in Oklahoma City. "We had a farm outside Boise City, Oklahoma, but we were dust-bowl Okies, blown all the way to Monterey Bay, California. Lost the farm. My Dad got work in a sardine cannery. We were dirt poor."

"Poor? You got nothin' on me when it comes to poor. I'm from a little place called Wolf's Bark, Miss-sippi, not even big enough to be called Mississippi. Wayne County, so poor we didn't even have Negroes."

Jim laughed. "What does that mean?"

"Means when the slaves got free, they high tailed it out of the backwoods for Chicago and Detroit and only the poor white trash were dumb enough to stay, like my family."

Jim looked past her and said, "Well, here comes your diddy-bopper."

"My, what?" She turned as Bogarde came into Hotsy Jazz.

"He bounces when he walks. See. Diddy-bop. Diddy-bop. Diddy-bop."

Bogarde bounced over, spotted Jim and let out a sigh as he moved up and put his hand on Desiree's shoulder.

"So how's the limp coming along?" Bogarde to Jim.

A blast of music accompanying the latest stripper drowned out Jim's, "Fuck you."

Desiree read the lips and climbed off the stool, purse in one hand, Bogarde's hand in the other as she pulled her boyfriend away from the bar-back. Bogarde made a feint as if to pull away and go for Jim, but she held on and his feint was just that. All bluff.

Leo moved up behind Jim as the two left the club. "One punch, right?"

"Half-a-left hook."

"Give him the right cross, right on the nose."

No doubt, Jim thought, he could floor the diddy-bopper but how would Desiree react? As he wiped his hands on a dish towel, he thought about it a little harder and suspected she might enjoy it a little. Did women really like men fighting over them? Like maybe from cave-men days. Or would she think Jim was a typical male brute. A beast. A gorilla.

His foot throbbed as he stepped away from the sink, reminding him it was there again – the unending pain.

• • •

Bogarde told her he'd run into Elmer. The smarty-pants didn't look so cocky now. "He was with a woman. Son-of-a-bitch recognized me too from Z Best. Never said a word about the stick up."

"What was he doing there?" They wove their way through the Bourbon Street crowd, though strong scents of cheap perfume, men's hair oil and enough cigarette smoke to cause a fog.

"He picked up a chippy at church."

"Why is he still in town?"

They had to separate to get through the crowd, Desiree stepping into the street, tip-toeing around the garbage in the gutter before getting back up on the banquette with Bogarde.

"Let's get off Bourbon." She led the way up a side street and asked, "Where are we eating?"

"I don't know." He sounded exasperated. "We'll find a freakin' diner."

"Don't take it out on me, mister. This was your master plan."

Bogarde stopped. "He was a goddamn *tourist!*"

"Not anymore." She kept walking fast and he had to catch up.

"Actually," Bogarde's smug voice was back. "I asked him, 'Aren't you from out of town' and he said he was heading back to Topeka on a morning flight. Then he kissed the chippy, a real porker and said he'd met a good woman and thought he'd stay the day. Then he rolled his eyes and said, 'Maybe the night', and the porker giggled. It was disgusting."

"Didn't say anything about losing five thousand dollars? Didn't even try to get the woman sorry for him."

"Not in front of me. But he asked about the Buick Century I sold a fat-ass couple on the Fourth of July. He was actually looking for a goddamn car."

They made it up to Bogarde's car parked up on Rampart.

"So where do you wanna eat?" Bogarde asked as they climbed in.

"Just take me home."

• • •

It was so humid already at eight in the morning, Jim's back was soaked by the time he got home. He took a cold bath and lay in the cool water for as long as he could stand it, took two more pain pills and went to bed, making sure the ceiling fan over the bed was on high. Directing the fan on his nightstand to make sure it oscillated back and forth across the bed.

He let his mind imagine him away from New Orleans, away from European battle scenes, all the way to a Caribbean nightclub where a girl was singing. He was sitting alone at a table and watched her as she sat on the piano, watched her through a fog of smoke.

No. No smoke. It was his daydream so he wiped away the smoke and watched Ava Gardner sing a torch-song about lost love. She wore the tight, sleeveless black dress and the long black glove on her right hand from *The Killers,* her black hair parted on the side, half-covering her left eye. She stared straight at Jim as she climbed off the piano, revealed a nice view of her thigh. She slinked over, moving smoothly, like a black panther. He stood up.

Jim wore a charcoal gray suit and there was no limp when he moved to her, took her in his arms. She stopped singing but the music played on, soft, low, sensual. She felt light in his arms and moved in perfect sync with him as the ceiling fan cooled his body and the oscillating fan made a rhythmic clicking, back and forth, back and forth. The pain pills clouded his mind, numbing the pain in his foot and he felt himself slip away.

Jim Munster dreamed but not of Ava Gardner, and thankfully, not of the exploding trees of the Hürtgen forest, nor even the long, dusty ride to the coast in the family's jalopy, watching his old man nurse that ancient Oldsmobile across the plains all the way to Monterey Bay. He dreamed of a high school prom, the one he didn't go to because only the kids with good clothes went to the prom.

He was seventeen again, standing outside the gymnasium as the band played Glenn Miller's *Moonlight Serenade*. A girl came out of the darkness. She wore a white dress, sleeveless but full and low cut, showing cleavage as she came up to him. She stopped in front of him and licked her red lips that glistened in the bright lights outside the gym.

Desiree looked different as a teen-ager, her eyes just as blue, her upper lip rising to a slight point, the lower lip a little fuller as she pursed them, inched closer and brushed her lips across his. She took his hand and led him into the prom. He wore the same charcoal suit and when they danced it was just as smooth and slow as the dance with Ava Gardner, only the press of Desiree's body against his was scintillating.

He felt it rolling through his body, felt the passion rising, felt her breath on his shoulder as they slow-danced. He felt her heart stammering against his chest as the dance went on and on. When the music stopped, they kept dancing, when the lights went up, they kept dancing, when the prom queen was announced, they kept dancing. When the prom ended and everyone was gone, including the band, and the lights went down, Jim and Desiree kept dancing. But Jim knew it was a dream, even while asleep, and knew it wouldn't last.

A blast of hot air that took his breath away and brought him to the Hürtgen to the trees exploding from strikes by high velocity artillery shells, long splinters of razor-sharp wood slicing through the shirts of the GIs hunkered down, men balled up into fetal positions as they tried to breathe, tried to wait out each round, tried to survive. He heard a man screaming and realized it was him.

Jim woke to the ceiling fan and closed his mouth, waiting for the landlady or a neighbor to bang on his door to tell him to shut up, but there was no bang. His breathing returned to normal and he looked at the clock. Ten-thirty. He'd slept maybe an hour. He gingerly moved his foot and there was no pain but the ceiling looked wavy and the pills were working. He shut his eyes tight and reached back for the dream, reaching back to the prom he never went to.

Chapter 5

DON'T TELL ME – THE CAMERAMAN IN THE CLOSET TRICK

As Jim Munster tried to get back to sleep around ten-thirty that Monday morning, Desiree Blanc walked into the main branch of the Whitney National Bank on Poydras Street, her pumps echoing on the marble floor. The bank was ornate, occupying the entire first floor of a five story office building, a big old stone building, the Whitney's trade-mark brass clock hanging outside. The lobby was huge with a row of ten tellers behind brass cages, only five stalls occupied at the moment. She went past the tellers, catching the eye of the security guard, an old timer with gray hair and a matching moustache. He tipped his bus driver cap to her as she arrived at the little wooden gate that separated the lobby from the carpeted area where the bank managers sat behind large desks.

The closest manager, a young man with red hair, looked up and smiled at her. "Can I help you?"

"I'd like to get into my safety deposit box." She held up her keys.

Desiree wore a black skirt, not too tight and not too short, but tight enough to draw the attention of the men whom she'd passed that morning. Her white blouse wasn't too sheer, but sheer enough to show the outline of her lacy French bra and low-cut enough to show some cleavage. She wore dark sunglasses and had teased out her hair again into a fluff, in case that pain-in-the-ass Elmer hadn't caught his flight out of town and just happened to be downtown that morning.

The manager asked for identification and she passed him her driver's license. He checked it as he flipped through a file of index cards, pulled one out and checked the signature against the one on the license. He returned her license and handed her the card, asking her to sign it, then dutifully checked the signatures again before bringing her to one of the two gigantic, walk-in safes. He unlocked the stainless steel gate and led her to a wall of safety deposit boxes. He used a key from his key chain and her key to unlock the twin locks on the box.

"There's a room for privacy," he said as he carried her deposit box to a nearby doorway. She followed him in and he put her box on the tiny wooden table inside and promptly left, closing the door behind him.

Desiree placed her purse up on the table, reached in and brought out an envelope. She counted the money again. Twenty-four hundred dollars exactly. She reached inside the deposit box and pulled out another envelope, the one she'd put in when she first got the box. There was three hundred dollars in Grants inside. She slipped both of the envelopes back in and closed the lid.

The manager was waiting outside the door and carried her box back to its slot, using both keys to lock it in. When he handed her keys back, his fingers brushed her hand. Their eyes met and his said in a low voice, "Haven't I seen you some place? You work around here?"

"No," she said, turned to leave, then turned back. "You might have seen me on the screen."

"Movies?" His green eyes lit up.

"Did you see *The Harvey Girls?* Came out last year." Desiree tapped down her glasses and looked over them. Leo told her in New Orleans, this was called *gleeking,* peeking over the top of glasses. "Starred Judy Garland, Angela Lansbury and Cyd Charisse. Won the academy award for best song – 'On The Atchison, Topeka and Santa Fe'."

"I know that song."

"Well I was in the chorus, had a couple lines." She pushed her glasses back up and walked away, feeling the manager and the guard watching her. As she stepped outside, a cop car passed and the coppers inside stopped at the corner, both watching her and she felt her throat clench. The prowl car turned the corner with the green light and she crossed the street, heading back toward the French Quarter.

Anger rose in her as she walked because she felt like such a country bumpkin. How could she be so dumb as to be spotted the other morning, walking in her red dress, the dress she wore to stick up Elmer? All the cops had to do when they had their meeting before the shift, what was it called? Roll call? All they had to do was put out a description of an ash blond in a red dress and the guys in that prowl car on Esplanade would go, "Hey, I think she lives in Marigny. We saw her."

OK, maybe Elmer hadn't gone to the cops for whatever reason. Maybe he'd absconded with the company funds himself. But she wasn't smart. She should have brought a rain coat, anything, to wear home.

As she moved down Carondelet Street, she had to dodge a car pulling out of a parking lot. The woman behind the wheel leaned on her horn and Desiree turned and shouted, "Pedestrians on the sidewalk have the right of way, you cow!"

Man, she was glad she hadn't told Bogarde about the cops on Esplanade. He thought she was dumb to begin with. By the time she reached Canal Street, Desiree decided she need a gun. She'd loved the feel of the grip of Bogarde's gun the other night, the weight of the gun, knowing the lethal bullets were inside. If she was going to be a gun-moll – no, she was a gun-moll – she wanted a gun. Not a big one like Bogarde's forty-five, but something smaller, something she could hold with one hand, one that'd fit in her purse. If they were going to stick up chumps, then she wanted her own gun. Bogarde said something about showing a gun to the guy in the bank he wanted to rob, then maybe she should be the one showing the gun. Who would suspect her?

She crossed behind a passing streetcar, careful to not catch her heel in the tracks, and wondered where she could get a gun. Leo would know, but did she want to ask? No way she'd ask Bogarde. He'd nix the idea.

She knew what she'd do as she reached the other side of Canal and proceeded up Bourbon Street. That's why God invented a little thing called The Yellow Pages.

• • •

At twelve-fifteen, Bogarde arrived outside the Chartres National Bank on Carondelet Street. If he'd been there earlier, Desiree would have walked right past him. He only had an hour for lunch and had used fifteen minutes to streetcar over, so he only took a few minutes checking the exterior of the bank, which looked like a small fortress, a narrow, two-story concrete building between much taller buildings with glass fronts. The bank had what looked like towers atop each corner and a parapet that ran along the rooftop.

The recessed front door, double doors, were arched and took a little strength to pull open. The floor was marble and there was a marble counter off to the left with cubby holes with bank slips inside. Two teller's windows faced the front doors and there was a customer at each and one customer standing in line next to a wooden railing. Off to the right was a low wall with three desks behind, each manned by a middle-aged fellow. Behind the desk closest to the vault sat balding, roly-poly James Gallagher, sans fake moustache. He was busy writing in a ledger.

Bogarde moved to the counter and started filling out a bank slip. He checked again and there was no guard. One of the tellers was a woman so he made sure to keep his back to her, lest she remembered what he looked like because he looked good that morning in his blue blazer, scarlet cravat with a baby blue shirt and white pants. He wore that get-up on purpose so his pain-in-the-ass boss would say something like he should have wore that on the Fourth of July, which was exactly what Jiminy barfed up as Bogarde arrived at work.

He left the bank with plenty enough time to pick up a po-boy around the corner from work and still get back in time. On the streetcar ride back up Canal, he formulated his plan on how he'd approach Desiree about sticking up that jewelry store. He'd talk her into it, but it would take a little work. Why was she always so difficult?

• • •

After work that night, Bogarde was waiting outside the dressing rooms and led Desiree right out of Hotsy. He was diddy-bopping big time as he pulled her through the crowd. She caught Jim's eye as she exited, raised a hand to wave and smiled at him. He gave her a slow wave back. Leo held up an icy club soda but she just shrugged and followed Bogarde out.

"What's the hurry?"

"We got a lot to talk about. I went to the bank today."

"What bank?"

He wheeled, eyes bulging. "The Chartres National Bank. The one where the mark works."

"What mark?"

He stopped and she said, "I'm just needling you. James Gallagher, right? Fake moustache? He was there tonight, front of the stage."

Bogarde shook his head and led her to his car, which he'd parked over on Dumaine Street. "They don't have a security guard at all," he said.

She was about to say the Whitney had, but something made her pause, kept her from telling Bogarde where her safety deposit box was. He was hiding his cash in coffee cans in his cupboard because he didn't trust banks.

"He'll be there tomorrow night for sure," Bogarde said as he unlocked his car door, then climbed in and reached over to unlock Desiree's. He took Dumaine up to Rampart and hung a left. "The wife's out of town."

"How do you know that?"

"Woman across the street. Bought a car from me and I've been using her house to spy on the Gallaghers and saw him pack up the wife and kids this evening in the station wagon and they had a lot of baggage. Couldn't be better for us." Actually Bogarde hadn't seen it at all. Fanny told him all about it when he went by there for supper.

Desiree nodded. "The woman across the street. She one of your middle-aged chippies?"

He took in a deep breath, staring straight ahead. "I told you I stopped doing that when we hooked up." He turned and gave her the hypnotic stare. "You don't trust me?"

Desiree stared back into his eyes and let hers go soft. She gave him a quivering smile and he bought it, looking back at the road and actually believed she believed him. He was getting goofier by the moment. She crossed her legs and looked out the side window. She wore her sleeveless white blouse and a tight, dark green skirt that didn't quite reach her knees. She had matching pumps.

"Tomorrow night, I'm going to sit with Gallagher," Bogarde went on, "and tell him I know you."

"He's probably seen us leaving Hotsy together."

"That's right. And I'll invite him to join us for drinks after, since he's so keen on meeting you."

"He is?"

"Don't you see the way he stares at you?"

"They all have the same stare."

Bogarde winked at her. "Yeah, but you're his blond desire." Bogarde liked to refer to the English translation of 'Desiree Blanc'.

"Then you slip him a note about meeting later. You'll tell him I'm not an attentive boyfriend and you get lonely and you play the field, whatever. Tell him sometimes a girl just wants a good time. Maybe a steak dinner. His wife's out of town and the woman of his sex dreams wants to spend a little time with him. It's perfect."

Yeah. As if anything was perfect.

They turned up Tulane and passed Charity Hospital on the left before taking a left on Claiborne Avenue.

"Then what?" asked Desiree.

"We get him into a hotel room and you strip down right away."

She closed her eyes, seeing it all now. "Don't tell me – the cameraman in the closet trick?"

"Yep. I'll be in the closet. You two get naked. Maybe start to play around and I'll come out and save the day. Whisk you away. Then we pay a visit to the bank, like a good couple only you need to see the vault to make sure your money's safe. I can still be your accountant."

"Investment lawyer." She cringed as Bogarde had to hit his brakes for a white car that crossed in front of him.

"Whatever. We go inside and fill the bags we'll bring with cash."

She kept from looking at him so he wouldn't see the disappointment in her eyes. "Is that when we show him the gun?"

"We may not need a gun."

Yeah, she thought. Gun-molls carry guns.

She turned to Bogarde as he took at left on Carrollton Avenue and headed toward the river. "Where are we going?"

"New place called The Camellia Grill."

She'd heard of it from Leo. Supposed to have the second best burgers in town, after the Clover Grill, but had the best milk shakes and the friendliest waiters.

"So we each carry in a bag and come out loaded."

"That's the idea."

"And what's he gonna tell them?"

"Young couple came in. He showed them the vault. They showed him a gun and took the money and told him if he didn't wait five minutes, they'd kill the two tellers." He patted her leg. "He can't tell the cops he knows you or I'll send the pictures to his wife."

"When are you going to tell him that?"

"In the vault."

She let it sit there a while as the car sped down the narrow avenue, beneath the boughs of huge oaks hanging overhead, streetcars on the small neutral ground on their left.

"Do we just tell him we're the 'beauty-and-the-beast gang'? So the gang'll get credit. You're not going to wear your gorilla mask."

"We'll just tell him. By then we'll be famous."

"Famous?" She didn't like the sound of this.

"Yeah, I didn't tell you about our little jewelry heist yet."

"What?"

• • •

They parked right in front of The Camellia Grill, which looked like a small version of a plantation house. Not Tara exactly but it had four white columns out front and a pitched room with a dormer above overlooking the avenue. Inside was a long counter shaped in a 'W' with stools, the grill and counter men on one side, customers and cash register on the near side. They were the only customers.

Two Negro waiters smiled at them as they entered. Bogarde moved them to the left and the smaller of the two waiters followed, bringing menus and glasses of water with shaved ice inside.

"I'm Harry," said the waiter, who looked young, twenty maybe. "Monday nights not our big night so your wishes are my desire."

Desire. Funny, thought Desiree.

"Say man," the other waiter called out from the grill, where a huge white man stood with a spatula in hand. "It's Tuesday morning, man.

"Oh, yeah." Harry smiled.

The placed smell faintly of flowers and Desiree wondered if it was camellia scented. The menu consisted of a long sheet of paper. Harry passed them each a pencil.

"Just check off what you want. Might I suggest the caviar or the escargot?"

"You have caviar?" asked Bogarde.

"No way, man. I'm just kiddin' around. But we got the most succulent burgers and the best milk shakes this side of the Vatican."

"Who told you that?" Desiree had to smile back at the man's big grin.

"Father Alphonses, a dean over at Loyola University just down the street." He meant St. Charles Avenue, of course. Even Desiree knew Tulane and Loyola were on St. Charles and The Camellia Grill was a half block up Carrollton from St. Charles. She was getting to know the city, all right.

They each ordered burgers and fries, Bogarde opting for a Coke while Desiree ordered a chocolate milk shake. She could afford a little treat. She'd skipped lunch. Harry took their orders to the cook and started on the Coke and milk shake, while the cook slapped burgers on the grill.

Desiree turned to her right and put her legs up on the next stool. She drew her right knee high and had to work her skirt up a little to get her knee up. Harry brought Bogarde's Coke and a fresh glass of water to her, handing them straws with the tip of the paper covering already open. When Desiree grabbed her straw, Harry pulled the covering away and did the same with Bogarde's straw.

When he looked at Desiree legs a second time, she realized he could see up her skirt. She'd slipped on white panties, so he was seeing a lot less than everyone had seen at Hotsy, and he moved away quickly, but it gave her a charge knowing he'd sneaked a peek.

Bogarde leaned against her back, which was to him, and whispered, "We'll talk about the jewelry thing in the car."

"OK," she whispered back as Harry returned to fill their water glasses from a pitcher. He didn't look at her legs until he was about to pull away and took another glance. The smell of cooking meat permeated the room and Desiree's stomach rumbled in response. She and Bogarde sat in the turn of the counter, so she was facing the turn. The big waiter came to wipe down the counter and got a peek up her skirt too.

Harry brought the burgers, fries and her chocolate shake which she'd watched him make from crushed ice, chocolate ice cream, milk and two different syrups. She took as sip and it was dreamy. At that moment two cops came in, a heavy-set one in his forties and a much younger one. They had a little silver '7' on the collars of their sky-blue police shirts. That would be the Seventh Precinct. The French Quarter cops wore a little '3' on their collars.

She was about to pull her leg down as the cops came to sit on the other side of the turn of the counter, the big guy positioning himself to look right up her skirt. She paused and thought about it as the cop took a long look, then the big waiter brought water and menus.

Why not give the cops a peek? Why not have the cops in the Seventh Precinct say, 'Yeah, we saw an ash blond beauty right here uptown. They're everywhere, man'? They'd see a lot more of her at Hotsy.

The burgers arrived and were as succulent as Harry described. The fries were a little skinny but the shake was so delicious Desiree only took small sips to make it last and used the two glasses of water to wash down her meal.

Bogarde remained quiet and she could feel his tenseness since the cops came in.

The young cop was peeking too so decided to give them something to talk about. She crossed her leg like a man, knee wide and toyed with the insole of her pump. She could feel them staring as she gave them a full view of her crotch. Harry came to take a peek but was careful the cops didn't see him.

Another couple came in and the cops instinctively turned to see so Desiree turned her knee around to Harry and let him have a good, long look, before winking at him and closing up her legs.

Bogarde was too busy eating and trying not to let the cops see his face to even notice. There was a big grin on Harry's face as Desiree finished the burger and the last fry, savoring the final sips of chocolate shake. She felt flushed, felt weird. She stripped for hundreds of men all the time but these clandestine peeks made her heartbeat rise. She got a kick out of flashing these guys because they all seemed so rapt in looking.

Bogarde snatched up the bill and Desiree left Harry a nice tip, winking at the man again as he thanked her with a wide grin.

"We need to come here again," she told Bogarde as they stepped to the car.

Next time she wouldn't wear panties.

•••

The rain started a block later and came in a rush, as if a fire hose was turned on them. Bogarde slowed the Ford, the wipers vainly trying to keep the windshield clear. But the raindrops were too fat and too frequent.

"It's called Roth Brothers Jewelers. A little place on Chartres, just past the Cathedral."

"And you want to pull a heist. A daylight heist because jewelers aren't open at night?"

"That's right, kiddo. I've got it all figured but I wanna show you the layout in case I missed something."

Yeah. Pick my brain. Doesn't admit I have a brain but knows he might have missed something.

A streetcar lumbered past, going their way and if a car was traveling slower than an electric streetcar, it was going way too slow. Bogarde gunned it and the back wheels spun before catching cement and they passed the streetcar.

"We in a hurry?"

"Not really."

They caught the light at Claiborne and Bogarde fudged, almost turning on the red light, but you never knew when a cop car was lurking and the NOPD pricks didn't mind getting out in the rain to write a damn ticket. Bogarde had two in the glove box and hadn't paid them yet. If the cops ever got efficient they'd make a killing collecting on all the outstanding tickets in this city full of bad drivers.

One of those bad drivers ran right though the red light at Tulane, but Bogarde saw him coming. Another thing, in New Orleans, when the light turned green you always waited a second or two to let the red light rushers blow past or you'd wind up with a Buick in the side of your car.

"It's a small place?" asked Desiree as they took a left on Rampart.

"Very small and settled back away from the sidewalk."

She wasn't about to correct him about banquette. She'd done it once and he needled her about the fact she really wasn't from New Orleans. As if he was. The rain stopped as suddenly as it started and the French Quarter streets were completely dry.

They turned down St. Ann Street and went all the way to Chartres where Bogarde took another left and slowed down. He couldn't find a parking stop, but pulled around the corner of an even narrower street called Madison.

"It's back there." He turned in the seat and she followed suit and it took a moment to see the place, which was all dark.

"Wonder why they don't keep a light on in case cops need to see inside," she said, "in case of burglars?"

"How do you know all that?"

"My daddy read detective magazines and so I read them."

"Didn't know your old man could read."

She shoved him and he chuckled.

"The place is run by two old men and I mean old. There's an aisle down the center of the store with glass cases on either side with a walkway behind each case. The way it's set back, no one can see inside unless they're right in front. We go in, me wearing the gorilla mask, you in a revealing outfit so you're just a sexy body and blond hair, wear dark sunglasses, and we stick up the place, take any loose gems, take some fancy jewelry and all the cash.

"We take the loot and run. Park the car here on Madison and hit Decatur, can go either way right out of the Quarter." Bogarde turned around and tooled the Ford down to Decatur Street where he took a quick left. "I got a license plate from a used Ford from the lot. The car won't ever sell so I'll stick the plate back on it and when el-cheepo Jiminy gets tired of seeing it, he'll wholesale it out to one of the dealers out in St. Bernard or Jefferson. Even if it's spotted, it ain't registered to me."

Bogarde told her, before they stuck up Elmer, that 'borrowing' one of the cars from Z Best was impossible as Jiminy took the keys to the cars home with him every night.

"We gotta tell them in the jewelry store we're the 'beauty-and-the-beast bang'. It'll make the papers."

"Why would you want to do that?"

"If I get caught I wanna go to jail famous. Don't you want to be famous?"

"I want to be rich."

"Same thing."

What was the use in arguing? Desiree reached over and played with Bogarde's arm. He looked at her and winked. "Feeling a little frisky? Me too. Your place or mine?"

On their way to Bogarde's, Desiree asked, "When are we going to stick up this place?"

"Friday."

"This Friday?"

"You got other plans?"

She'd better get her gun fast.

• • •

The sex was good at least. Maybe it was better because she wasn't in love with Bogarde, not that she'd ever been in love. They both knew it, but they both enjoyed the coupling, Desiree more that evening and she wondered if it had anything to do with flashing those guys in The Camellia Grill. She knew her sex drive was a chemical thing, a hormonal thing and sometimes she just had to have it. Sometimes, she felt like she was in heat, like an alley cat and she knew better. Humans didn't go into heat. Well, maybe the doctors didn't have it all figured out yet because sometimes Desiree wanted to actually jump a man.

She thought Bogarde was falling asleep as they lay on their backs on his bed, the ceiling fan blowing air over their damp bodies, until he said, "I wanna ask you something and I don't wanna piss you off about it."

"Go ahead."

"You weren't a virgin when we hooked up, not that virgins are worth a damn. But how'd you loose yours? I lost mine to a babysitter, an older woman."

"That's no surprise," Desiree said. "I lost mine to a country boy from high school. Back of his pickup truck."

"Did your old man or your uncles ever, you know, try anything with you? I mean you being the prettiest girl ever came outta Wolf's Howl, Mississippi.

"Wolf's Bark and no way. My daddy was a peanut farmer, still is and my uncles are farmers too, worked the soil. They all treated me like I was made a porcelain. I was their princess. None of my relatives, not even my cousins would ever touch me. So no, I'm not one of those girls who got molested as a child and ran away to the big city."

She sat up and pulled her legs off the bed.

"I told you. This is just a stop over for me on my way to Hollywood."

"Right." His voice was fading and his eyes closed now. When he'd asked about her just then the smart-ass was missing from his voice. It was as if he really cared. When they made love that evening, it was just as fierce but sometimes the man made Desiree feel as if she really meant something to him.

As she dressed, she watched him sleep and realized he'd meant something to her at first, something strong, something emotional. It was still there, but not as strong and they both knew it was temporary.

"You see," she told her sleeping boyfriend. "My daddy thinks I'm pure. Always will. He's the only man who'll ever love me without wanting anything back." She dug a scarf out of her purse and locked the door on the way out of Bogarde's place.

• • •

The French Quarter was different at three in the morning, especially during the week, especially away from Bourbon Street. Desiree didn't want to go straight home and headed toward Decatur Street where the coffee shops, like the bars on Bourbon, were always open. She smelled rain in the air again but it wasn't raining yet. The air seemed lighter with and an almost cool breeze floated in from the river, bringing scents of the big muddy Mississippi water.

Desiree cut through Pirate Alley to get down to Chartres Street and Jackson Square, the black wrought iron railing of St. Anthony's Garden on her left, the townhouses along the alley on her right. The cobblestone alley was slanted to its center where a drain ran and she had to watch her step in the darkness.

A voice startled her and she stopped as a man called out, "Puss. Puss! Here Puss – Puss." The voice had a Mississippi accent and she saw its owner as he stepped out from the alley that ran into Pirate Alley from the next street.

"Oh, excuse me, ma'am," he said as he stopped under a dim streetlight. "I beg your pardon, but have you seen a cat? My Puss is out on the town and I'm afraid she'll run into trouble." He was a short man with curly brown hair, receding, and wore a small moustache. He was in a white shirt and white pants and was barefoot.

She could smell liquor on his breath as she stepped into the light.

"This is no place for you either, miss. The night is full of tom cats." He swayed a little. "I, of course, am not one of that breed. I am a southern gentleman and if you'll allow me to escort you through the remainder of this alley, I would be grateful. If not, then I'll just study the way you move and put it on paper."

"What are you, a reporter?"

He laughed and had to hold on to the light post. It took almost a minute for him to recover. When he did he looked back up the alley and said, "Do you know that building at 624 Pirate Alley, the one with the two balconies overlooking St. Anthony's Garden?"

Desiree looked back, saw the townhouse but just shrugged.

"I'll have you know William Faulkner wrote his first novel up there. There's a plaque on the wall. Have you ever read Mr. Faulkner?"

He was cute, in a feminine sort of way and didn't look the least bit dangerous.

"As a matter of fact, I'm from north Mississippi like Mr. Faulkner and I've read almost everything he's written." She took a step closer. "I like his short stories best of all, 'A Rose for Emily' is my favorite."

The man stood up straighter and said, "Well, well. A fellow Mississippian. Allow me to introduce myself. I'm Thomas." He stuck out his hand to shake and Desiree shook it.

"I'm Desiree."

"Of course you are," he said. "If you are not the epitome of desire, it does not exist."

Desiree took the scarf off her head and shook out her hair.

"My. My. You are far too pretty for my play. I'm writing about an aging woman and her slimy brother-in-law. I'm writing it around the corner on St. Peter Street. One day, they just might put a plaque on the wall there, what do you think?"

"Why not?"

Thomas put his hand over his mouth and tried to suppress a belch. Recovering, he asked, "Will you have a drink with me?"

"Coffee," she said. "I'm heading to Café Du Monde."

"Coffee it is." Thomas stuck out an elbow. Desiree hesitated, looking into the man's soft eyes, then took it.

He wasn't as drunk as he seemed and walked with no problem.

"This is one of my favorite places on planet Earth." He waved at the wrought iron fence surrounding Jackson Square. "It inspires me."

"You're writing about Jackson Square?"

"Lord no, the lower Quarter is where I'm setting my play, where the working people live. The ones who occupy these apartments," he waved to the red brick apartment houses on either side of the square as he spoke, "they are idlers, living off the family fortune. Did you know these are the oldest apartment houses in North America?"

"No."

"They weren't always as expensive to live as now. The writer Sherwood Anderson lived there. Have you read Mr. Anderson?"

"I don't think so."

The skirted the square and turned down St. Ann for the café. The breeze picked up and the large leaves of the banana trees and thick leaves of the magnolias danced in the square. It sounded like waves washing to shore, like in the movies. Desiree had never seen an ocean, not even the Gulf of Mexico, but she would when she got to Hollywood.

There were six customers sat at small table beneath the green-and-white striped awning of Café Du Monde. Desiree was about to sit at a table when Thomas said, "Inside. The rain won't get us there."

They went into the brightly lit café that smelled of strong coffee and powered sugar. Just as they sat, the rain hit, washing in with a brisk breeze, driving the outside customers inside, the awning unable to protect them from a driving rainstorm. Desiree and Thomas sat at one of the tables against the windows facing Decatur Street. Desiree ordered café-au-lait. Thomas ordered beignets along with his café-au-lait and when they arrived, an order of three, he offered one to Desiree who shook her head.

"You must have an intense inner strength in order to resist these," he said before taking a large bite of beignet, powdered sugar dotting his moustache.

"Beside an aging woman and a slimy man, what's your play about?"

Thomas put a finger over his lips and shushed her. "The Russians could be listening," he quipped, then sat up straighter. "I've said too much already. A writer should write first, then talk about it after. I know dozens of playwrights and want-to-be novelists who keep telling me what they are going to write and never write it."

They both took sips of coffee and she saw he watched her carefully as if he was studying her. This was a man who could handle his liquor, no doubt.

"What do you do, Mademoiselle Desiree? If I may be so bold to ask?

"I work on Bourbon Street."

"A dancer, singer?"

"Stripper."

He leaned so far back, he almost fell over, his eyes lighting up as if he was struck by lightning. "No doubt, you bring the house down with your act."

"Hardly." She drank more coffee.

"Carnality, child, is where we all came from and where we all want to return." Thomas finished off the first beignet and started on the second. "They are better," he said with a mouthful, "when hot."

The rain slammed against the windows and Desiree figured the uptown shower finally made it to the Quarter. A loud horn echoed from a ship just beyond the sea wall, turning both that way.

"I'm waiting for one of them to slice through the levee and flood the entire Quarter."

Desiree finished her coffee and so did Thomas, who ordered two more as he ate his final beignet.

"What about your cat?"

"She'll find a nice warm spot to curl up and come home in the morning for food. I try to keep her inside all the time, but she's her own woman."

She wanted to ask if this was his first play, but something told her it wasn't. Something told her this was not only a successful playwright, but probably an important one.

"May I have an autograph?" she said, pulling out the small note pad she always kept in her purse.

"Of course," said Thomas and he signed it to 'Desiree of Pirate Alley. I will never forget our meeting, Tennessee Williams'.

"Tennessee Williams?" She'd heard the name. "But you're from Mississippi."

"Who wants to be called Mississippi Williams?" Thomas laughed. "My fraternity brothers nicknamed me Tennessee and it looks much better on paper than Thomas." He pointed to Desiree's note pad. "Now, if you would indulge me with your autograph, I would be immensely proud."

She wrote 'To Thomas of Pirate Alley and signed it Desiree Blanc'. She wanted to add, 'the epitome of desire' but wasn't sure of the spelling of epitome. Thomas seemed delighted at the autograph.

"This play, of course, will be my swan song because I am dying." He said with a smile.

She gave him a long look. "You're not serious."

He seemed to think about it and said, "I'm not sure."

"Well, before you die you need to come see me take off my clothes. I'm at Hotsy Jazz on Bourbon." She jotted down her schedule for the next two weeks, not wanting him to drop in when she was off. "I work four p.m. until midnight."

"I shall do that. Without fail. May I bring my boyfriend?"

Jim shook his head as he read the short article again.

"They had a cover story ready pretty quickly, didn't they?" Leo went on. "When did you ever know the military to figure things out so quickly?"

"Never."

"No way the sheriff and that major mistook aluminum foil, tape and pieces of rubber for a flying saucer," Leo said. "It's a cover up, just like the firebombing of Dresden."

"The what?" Jim went back to washing glasses. Desiree took another sip of the club soda that was so icy, it chilled her throat.

"During the war," Leo explained, "the Germans declared Dresden an open city. Kept the lights on at night, let refugees congregate there, even brought in POWs. Well, the US Army Air Corps decided it was a good idea to destroy the city, which included some of the most beautiful Medieval cathedrals in Europe, gothic architecture we'll never see again. Hand-made cathedrals. The Air Corps thought it would demoralize the Germans so on Valentine's Day, 1945, they firebombed the city, created a firestorm so intense it burned the entire atmosphere in the city. Burned all the oxygen. That's what put out the fire.

"We did the same thing to Tokyo, but those were Japanese. You know, the yellow people who started the war. But Dresden were white people, Germans and refugees from all over Europe, not to mention hundreds of American POWs who got incinerated.

"Ever hear anything about this?"

Jim and Desiree shook their heads.

Desiree said, "Why different because they were white people?"

"No difference," Leo went on. "Except to the U.S. Government who are keeping it a secret. They think it's different. My buddy's son, Kurt, was one of seven POWs who lived. He's going to write a book about it, but can't right now because it's still classified. He's working as a police reporter in Chicago. The carnage he described after the firebombing is the worse I've ever heard. So you think the Air Force knows how to cover up a story, or what?"

Leo went off to serve two impatient customers.

"Well, that put a damper on the evening," said Desiree.

Jim looked confused.

Desiree put an elbow up on the bar and cupped her chin in the upturned palm of her hand and said, "Why do you work here? You could do better."

Jim didn't look up from the dishwater as he said, "I like to look at the naked girls." He looked up with a big smile.

She reached over and pinched his arm.

"Actually," he said. "Leo's teaching me the bartender trade. Meanwhile, I get paid to watch you strip off your clothes."

"You don't clock in until midnight, mister. You come in early to see me."

He wiped off his hands with a towel and gave her that same shy smile he'd given her back at Wit's End Diner. When was that? Only four days ago. She sure felt like she knew this guy longer.

"Come in early? Guilty," he said.

Desiree finished her club soda and passed on a second. Before leaving she went back into the dressing room for a quick fresh-up of her make-up before leaving Hotsy. She had to re-apply her lipstick after drinking the club soda. Toni Two-Lane was on stage and a man was howling like a wolf when she came back out. Desiree was going to go tell Jim and Leo 'bye' but two of Baddie's men cut in front of her and snatched up the howler.

She realized one of the men was Turtle, who spied her and grinned at her. Gave her a "How ya doin'," as they hustled the howler out of Hotsy. She followed them out as they cleared away the crowd.

Jim watched Desiree leave. Leo put an elbow up on Jim's shoulder. "Ever read any good science-fiction stories?" Leo asked.

"Not really."

"I'll bring you some magazines. You'll like them."

"Magazines?" said Jim. "But it's not real."

"Fiction is a lot better than reality, son."

• • •

The brass plaque outside the Old Absinthe House Bar in the three hundred block of Bourbon Street said the building was built in 1806 and was a fine example of a Creole Entresol commercial-residential building with an intermediate floor and lighted by fanlight transoms over the doors. It also mentioned the balcony.

Before going in, Desiree glanced up at the fine, black wrought iron balcony, more intricate than most.

She unbuttoned two buttons on her blouse, went inside and stopped immediately. It felt as if she'd stepped back into time, the bar looking like a movie set of an 1890s saloon with bright red wall-paper behind an old wooden bar, wooden posts supporting exposed beams and shelves of liquor in front of mirrors that ran the length of the bar.

She spotted Bogarde and the mark sitting at the marble bar. James Gallagher was sweating so much he had to wipe his forehead with a handkerchief that looked already damp. His fake moustache dangled under his nose. Desiree stepped up and pulled the moustache off, dropping it on the bar.

"You won't need that," she said. Then she leaned close, their lips almost touching. She licked her lips and sat on the stool next to Gallagher. She told the bartender, "Club Soda, please."

"Why ... why ... not try an absinthe?" Gallagher asked.

"I thought it was illegal."

"It is." Gallagher tried to wink but it looked more like a butterfly's wings batting wildly. "It's illegal in America. But this is New Orleans."

Bogarde leaned around Gallagher and showed her a fancy looking wine glass with a creamy green liquid inside. "The French call it *The Green Fairy*," said Bogarde as he took a sip. "Smooth as silk." Gallagher had two of the same glasses in front of him on the bar, both empty.

Desiree cancelled her club soda and ordered an absinthe. The bartender, a thick man with a pock-marked face and bright red hair showed her how the drink was prepared.

"Ya' don't just drop it in a glass," the bartender said as he put an empty glass, identical to Bogarde's, on the bar in front of Desiree. He poured bright green liquid from a dark bottle into the glass until it reached a notch in the glass, about a third of the way up. He placed a silver spoon with a hole in it atop the glass and put a sugar cube in the bowl of the spoon and slowly poured ice-cold water over the sugar cube letting it dissolve. The liquid was a cloudy pale green now.

"That smell," said the bartender as he lifted the drink for Desiree to sniff, "is anise, a licorice, and fennel, wormwood and star anise. The water allows the herbs to blossom and brings out the scents that are normally overpowered by the anise." He handed the glass to Desiree who took a small sip. Sweet with a kick of an after-taste.

As the bartender backed away, he added, "When it was legal, we used to make frappé, letting ice-water, sugar and absinthe mix in a slow drip from a fountain."

It tasted so good, Desiree slowed down lest she drink it all at once. She didn't like getting drunk. The only times she had, she'd suffered terrible hangovers.

Gallagher and Bogarde ordered another absinthe and Desiree watched the bartender prepare theirs.

"Why is it illegal?" she asked.

Gallagher wanted to answer, but only managed a noise that sounded something like a dog trying not to growl. Bogarde just shrugged. The bartender said, "it's dangerously addictive and produces a chemical called thujone in the human body that is psychoactive, causes delirium, hallucinations."

Desiree wasn't sure what all that meant, but it didn't sound good. One absinthe would be her limit.

Bogarde finished his drink first, climbed off the stool and said, "Gotta go. Got a date." He winked at Desiree, then said, "Oh yes, Desiree Blanc – this is your biggest fan, Mr. James Gallagher. You two have fun now." He hurried out and Desiree took another sip of her drink as Gallagher downed his.

He ordered another and Desiree ordered a club soda when she finished hers, a few silent minutes later.

Gallagher finally said, "I, uh, um, your act is, um, uh, incredible."

"How?" Desiree put her elbow up on the bar, again resting her chin in the open palm of her hand and smiled at the mark.

"Oh, um, uh, you're skin, uh, is so. It shines. So white and creamy."

"Well, thank you." She sat back and said, "Did you have supper?"

"Huh? Me? No. Did you?"

"No and I feel like a steak. But where can we get one after midnight?

His eyes lit up. "I know just the place. It's uptown."

Bogarde better be shadowing them, and if he was, he was good at not being spotted. She walked next to Gallagher and the man shuffled as he walked, kept looking at her as if he didn't believe she was there next to him.

"So, you're from the city," she said as they moved up Conti Street away from Bourbon.

"I, went uh, went to Jesuit. Where'd you, uh, go to, uh. School?"

"Buckatunna High School in Wayne Country, Miss-sippi. The Buckatunna Broncos."

"Uh. Jesuit. Um. Uh, Blue Jays."

Gallagher drove a black Mercury. Four doors with a big chrome grill in front and white-wall tires. As she slid in, Desiree noticed it was a Mercury Monterey. Didn't Jim say he'd lived on Monterey Bay, California?

Gallagher got in and started up the super-quiet engine to tool the big car uptown. He only rolled over two curbs and she was glad he kept the speed down, with all that absinthe in him. He took her to a restaurant on Claiborne Avenue, a one story masonry building with a neon sign above its door announcing it's name: T. Pittari Restaurant.

The dining room wasn't small but cozy with thick carpet and drapes. There were ten tables, all filled, even at two a.m. on a Wednesday. She noticed the waiters were older men, the place smelling wonderfully of cooked meat, the walls and carpet immaculately clean, but the menu was ... strange. Under 'steaks' – it listed venison, buffalo, gazelle, kangaroo and elk. Under 'smaller cuts' – it listed Alpine marmot, nutria and eastern grey squirrel. She'd eaten enough squirrel as a kid. Under 'seafood' – it listed grouper, tiger shark, hammerhead and sting ray. Under 'exotic' – it listed rattlesnake, monitor lizard and tapir.

"Tapir?" she asked incredulously when Gallagher explained the South American animal, only stuttering a little.

He nodded and said, "You, uh, know. I almost never stutter."

She reached over and patted his hand. The waiter asked if they'd like an appetizer as he took a quick peek at her cleavage. Gallagher ordered for them. Escargot. She knew that was snails but she'd never had it, so she'd give it a try. It came quickly and tasted pretty good, probably because of all the garlic. She noticed a couple men checking her out, but this was an uptown crowd and their looks were brief and half-hidden. The women more openly stared. None were young.

Gallagher settled on a gazelle steak and she went as far as to order buffalo, which was beef, after all. He ordered a bottle of Beaujolais. She didn't want to mix anything with the absinthe except Club Soda, so that's what she ordered. Gallagher leaned over to tell her the bald headed man and the chubby woman walking around were the owners, Mr. and Mrs. Tom Pittari. Italians.

"We should have ordered the elk lasagna," Gallagher added.

She began to wonder about Gallagher, a married man didn't mind being seen in public with another woman, even without his fake moustache. Was he being reckless or was it the absinthe? He drank two glasses of wine before the main course and four during it, his eyes growing redder the more he drank.

The buffalo steak was the most tasty piece of cooked meat she'd ever eaten. It was a filet cut with a slice of bacon around it. At least she hoped it was bacon, but wasn't about to ask. Gallagher insisted she try a bite of his gazelle and it was also very tasty. She had fried sweet potatoes with her filet while he had some sort of mashed carrots.

"Would you like some chocolate covered ants for dessert?" their waiter asked. He'd positioned himself to look down her blouse and he did. No ants, she thought, only Gallagher said yes and they came, looking like small chocolate covered raisins, one of her favorite candies when she splurged, which rarely happened.

"Crunchy," Gallagher said as he munched them. "You. Uh, um have to, uh, try it at least."

She did and they were crunchy and the milk chocolate very smooth only there was an after-taste that made her finish off her Club Soda quickly.

There was an awkward moment, standing outside the Mercury after supper, the street so quiet and dark with only streetlights at the corners as all the houses in the area were dark. Gallagher looked like he was about to lean over and try to kiss her, but he took in a deep breath and then another and teetered, and slowly fell back across the hood of his Mercury.

Now what?

Desiree stepped closer and he went, "Thewww. Thewww." It was a snore, of sorts.

Dammit to hell. She looked up the block at T. Pittari's. They'd been the last couple to leave but the waiters were still in there. She could call a cab. She started that way and a car engine cranked up. It took a second to recognize the Ford as it came out of a parking spot. Bogarde stopped in the middle of the street, got out and said, "Let's put him in the Mercury."

They put Gallagher in the back seat, rolled the windows down and left him there.

"What did he have to drink in there?" asked Bogarde, as they pulled away in the Ford.

"An entire bottle of wine."

"And absinthe. Man, is he going to have a helluva hangover."

• • •

As they left Hotsy Jazz shortly after eight a.m., Leo insisted Jim stop by his place for some of those magazines. It was on the way, so Jim stopped in. Leo lived on Bourbon but in the residential part in the lower French Quarter where the buildings were crumbling and the rent cheap.

The magazines were digest size and Jim glanced at the covers as he walked home. His foot didn't hurt at the end of the day. He'd been on it all day and the stiffness had worn away, so it was no problem walking. Only the sun came peeking through the buildings and was hot already on his face.

At home, he turned the fans up and got down to his skivvies and climbed into bed. He'd get a newspaper when he work up. For a moment he thought of Desiree again in that red skirt and blouse with her nipples hard.

He scooped the magazines off the end table.

Amazing Stories had a green, alien city on its cover, buildings built in the image of some Buddha-like giants. A red hovercraft, shiny and round, raced in front of the buildings with a blue craft behind firing lasers. Ah, a car chase on an alien word. On the lower right corner was 'The Indest Chase. The Most Sensational Story Ever Told'.

The cover of *Astounding Science-Fiction* had a guy in a silver space-suit, helmet in one hand, ray gun in another as he stood on stainless steel stairs descending from spaceship. Next to the guy was the name 'Skylark Smith' and in the lower left corner, 'Grey Lensman by E.E. Smith, Ph.D'.

Startling Stories, now that was a cover. A young man in a red spacesuit was being pulled away by a silver robot with one large eye and steel tentacles while a blond-haired maiden in a bathing suit top that looked like a lacy brassiere and a short blue skirt reached for the man. In the lower left corner was 'The Isotope Man by Harley Roberts', while on the right side was written 'Against The Fall of Night, a novel of the future by Arthur C. Clarke'.

He opened *Startling Stories* and let the pages take him away.

The first story, "The Bray Encounter" by F. K. Weasel began with ..."What Joe heard was a whirling sound reverberating through the open window of his bedroom. He looked out at the bright yellow, Kansas wheat field outside as the sound grew in intensity. Joe went to the window and saw it hovering over the field, sunlight reflecting off its golden surface ..."

Chapter 7
I NEED PROTECTION

Clavin's Gun Shop was on Friscoville Avenue, just off the St. Claude Avenue streetcar line in St. Bernard Parish, southeast of the city limits. It was in an old neighborhood called Arabi, mostly residential, but Friscoville was a mix of houses, businesses and warehouses down the block toward the river. Desiree, in dark sunglasses, a sky blue sundress and matching heels, climbed up the front porch of the wooden building that was once a house but now had a big sign covering its front windows that read: *Guns. Ammo. And More Guns.*

A tall man with black hair looked up from behind the counter, his eyes widening a little as she came in. She was the only customer at ten a.m., just as the place opened. She stopped in the doorway and looked around. The place smelled of gun oil, its walls lined with rifles, shotguns, bows and arrows. Two glass cases ran down either side of the place, each filled with handguns.

"Well, well. What can I do for you, little lady?"

Desiree took off her sunglasses as she sauntered to the counter and said, "I need protection."

"You tellin' *me?*"

She gave him a smile and said, "I want a handgun. Small enough to fit in this purse," she held up her white clutch bag, "big enough to drop a man with one shot."

"Cal Clavin, at your service."

He moved around the backside of the counter to one of the side counters, reached under the glass and pulled out a small square pistol.

"Twenty-five caliber semi-automatic ..." Clavin started but she cut him off.

"I don't want a pop gun. I want something bigger."

He shrugged, put the square pistol back and moved along of the case. He reached in and pulled a slightly bigger pistol. "This is a twenty-two – long " He held up his hand. "Very lethal. The bullets are small but they bounce around inside and tear up the organs."

Desiree put an impatient hand on her hip. "I don't want bouncing bullets. I want stopping power."

Clavin smiled broadly and threw up his hands. "OK. Over there." He pointed to the glass case on the other side of the room. He hurried around just as two men wearing cowboy hats came in, stopped immediately and took off their hats.

"Damn Cal," the older of the two said. "You sure spruced up the place."

The younger one guffawed. He actually went, "Guffaw, guffaw," as he checked out Desiree. She acknowledged them with a nod and turned to Clavin who pointed down at a gun like Bogarde's.

"A forty-five automatic. Stopping power to spare but it's too big for your purse and probably for your hand." He moved over to a row of pistols with round cylinders. "I recommend a thirty-eight caliber revolver." He reached in for a black pistol, took it out, opened the cylinder and handed it to her.

It had a smooth grip, mother of pearl and felt heavy enough.

"The bullets go right in the cylinder," Clavin said.

"How do you close it?"

He reached over and shut the cylinder. "Never point any gun at anyone, even if it's unloaded, unless you plan to kill him." He directed her hand to point at the rear wall. "Pull the trigger." He tapped the rear top of the gun. "You don't have to cock the hammer. It's double action."

She pulled the trigger, watching the hammer go back and then snap as it fell forward.

"Kind of stiff trigger pull," she said, handing it back to Clavin. "My Daddy had a twenty-two rifle and the trigger was much smoother."

As Clavin put the pistol back, she pointed at a silver one that looked a little bigger. "That's a thirty-eight?"

"Yes, ma'am. Colt Detective Special." He drew out the Colt. "Nickel-plated with a beveled wooden grip." He opened the cylinder, showed her it was empty and handed it to Desiree who closed the cylinder, pointed it at the head of a deer on the back wall and pulled the trigger. A lot smoother.

"Cock it."

"Huh?"

"Pull the hammer back with your thumb and it'll cock."

She did.

"Now squeeze the trigger slowly."

She aimed again and when the hammer fell it surprised her it was so easy.

"How much?" she said, still aiming at the deer's nose.

"One hundred – even," Clavin said, reaching into the glass case for the box the Colt had been resting in. "This one's brand new. Never been fired."

"Is it accurate?"

"It's a snub-nose. Two inch barrel. For close-up shooting but it's accurate. It's a Colt."

"Where's the safety?"

The cowboys snickered but Clavin just said, "Revolvers don't have safeties." He cocked the hammer. "You can drop it, slam it on the ground, beat it with a hammer but until you pull the trigger it won't fire. You have to pull the trigger." He waved to the case across the room. "You drop an automatic and it can go off. That's why they have safeties."

Desiree took the Colt back and pulled the trigger. "What type of ammo would you suggest?"

Clavin gave her his biggest smile yet. "This way, please."

"Is there a place where I can fire it? Like a shooting gallery."

"You mean a pistol range," said the older cowboy. He explained about a couple ranges, one out there in St. Bernard Parish and one on the other side of the city in Jefferson Parish. She watched Clavin as he put two boxes of ammunition on the counter. He explained she should buy one box to practice with and another, more expensive ammo to keep in the gun.

She paid cash, slipped six rounds into the Colt before putting in her purse and walked out with the boxes of ammo, the cowboys and Clavin watching her hips as she left. She liked the feel of the Colt. It wasn't too heavy and the checkered wooden grip felt comfortable in her hand.

And so the gun-moll now had a Colt .38 Detective Special tucked in her purse.

She itched to shoot it.

• • •

Seated on a wooden stool at the marble counter beneath the bright incandescent lights of Morning Call Coffee Stand, Jim Munster read a follow-up story in the *Santa Fe Pueblo* about a reporter's hushed conversation with a shaken mortician at Amundiga's Funeral Parlor in Artesia, New Mexico, forty-five miles south of Roswell. The mortician declared he had encountered three thin, hairless bodies that were anything but human. These remains were brought to the funeral parlor by two green U.S. Army hearses.

It was two days before the Roswell crash story hit the newspapers. The mortician described slanted eyes, even more slanted than Chinese eyes. Skin a pale green hue. Wide hands with six long fingers and a prehensile thumb, like a human's.

"I re-assembled the three bodies because they were torn apart." The mortician, who has seen many auto crash victims, the injuries to the alien bodies were consistent with a high speed crash. "I cleaned the bodies, " claimed the mortician. "But two army pathologists arrived and performed autopsies before the bodies were iced down and returned to the hearses and taken away."

The bodies were five and a half feet long and weighed maybe one hundred thirty pounds each. There was no clothing accompanying the bodies, no spacesuits, and the bodies were fairly clean except for some grass, dirt and debris embedded in the 'sea-foam green' bodies.

The reporter managed to locate four additional eye-witnesses in Artesia, three men and a woman, who saw the army hearses parked outside Amundiga's Funeral Parlor. The woman was a waitress at nearby Amoody's Diner, while one of the men was a peace officer, a former Marine who'd fought in the Pacific.

Jim got goose bumps reading the story, and read it again. Maybe he was getting too excited about this. Maybe reading those science-fiction stories made everything more credible. But this was a *newspaper* article from the associated press.

He'd read through the entire issue of *Startling Stories,* and the stories were so damn good, especially "The Isotope Man." It was fiction of course, but the writer did such a great job. An experiment gone awry which turned into a chase story across a distance solar system. The silver robot with one large eye and steel tentacles was chillingly menacing. The romance between the blond-haired maiden in the lacy brassiere and a short blue skirt and the spaceman actually worked well as Jim was pulling for them. He was so awake when he finished the story he read on until he finished the magazine.

The *Santa Fe Pueblo* promised drawings of the aliens in their next edition.

Jim downed the rest of his coffee and glanced at the wall clock. Almost three p.m. Time to get ready for work. The waiter asked if he wanted another but three extra strong coffees were enough for Jim.

"Don't see many people drink it black," said the young waiter.

"It's more like espresso," Jim said, climbing off the stool. Only there was a different aftertaste from this strong coffee, almost smoky.

He felt the familiar needles of pain in his ankle and limped into the hot afternoon sunlight. He smelled the mud from the river now and watched the masts of a ship passing beyond the sea wall. This was his last shift before two days off. He'd check the movies of course but he'd also check the newsstand over on Canal Street for the current issues of *Starling Stories, Amazing Stories, Astounding,* whatever he could find.

He was on a roll now, managing the pain in his foot, his mind occupied. If only he could get to know Desiree a little better ...

• • •

In the middle of her last act, as she rolled her ass toward the crowd, Desiree thought about where she could go shoot the Detective Special. New Orleans was surrounded by woods, but it was mostly swamp and the last thing she wanted to do was come across a gator, worse would be a cottonmouth water moccasin. She'd heard stories about cottonmouths back home. Unlike a rattlesnake, which would bite you once, saving its venom for small prey, a cottonmouth would strike you again and again because it was just plain evil.

She's thought of maybe asking Mr. Badalamente, but something told her she didn't want him to know she had a gun. No way she could ask Bogarde. He's just put her down. Why does a broad need a gun? She'd rather surprise him when she pulled it out on the next job. Maybe she'd ask Leo.

The set ended and she realized she hadn't seen James Gallagher that evening at all. When was his wife coming back into town? When she went back out, she didn't spot Bogarde and went to the bar where Leo had her club soda waiting and Jim was washing glasses again. She sat across from him and gave him a wink. Jim's arms were wet up to the elbows and she watched the thick muscles flex as he worked.

Leo moved off to wait on customer and she and Jim just looked at each other as she took sips and he finished and dried his hands and arms with a white towel. He wiped the bar down, reaching over to move her purse, stopping for a second.

"What's in here?"

The Colt. She cringed and pulled the purse back to her.

His eyes narrowed. "What is it?"

She leaned over and said, "I bought a gun."

"Really? Why would you … never mind. This is New Orleans."

"Jimbo!" Leo called out and Jim turned to him. "Jax and Miller High Life."

Jim waved, backed away from Desiree and said, "Cooler time." He went to the side and reached into the coolers, drawing out two cases of Jax Beer and two cases of Miller. He carried them two cases at a time and his muscles rippled. He asked as he passed, "You just got it?"

She nodded.

On his way back he said, "You shoot it yet?"

She shook her head.

He came right back with the second two cases. "You wanna go shoot it?"

"Yeah."

When he'd put away the beer, he came back but looked past her and his face went disappointed. She turned as Bogarde came through the door.

She looked back at Jim. "You know a place I can shoot it?"

"I can take you."

She grabbed her purse as she climbed off the stool. "We're off tomorrow. Can you meet me at Morning Call?"

"I can be there in the morning."

She smiled. "Let's try one o'clock. We both need to sleep in." She caught Bogarde before he reached the bar, took his hand and led him out.

Jim watched them, thinking, yeah like he'd be able to sleep in.

As soon as they got outside, Bogarde growled in her ear, "Gallagher's goddamn wife came back."

They ducked up a side street, away from Bourbon, heading toward Rampart Street. It smelled much worse tonight, more garbage than usual out on the narrow street. She thought she saw a rat next to a building, but it turned out to be a small gray cat.

She pulled her hand away and slowed down. "So the fool's wife came home."

Bogarde wheeled. "Timing! Timing's everything in a heist. That's what ruined Dillinger, Bonnie and Clyde, Baby Face Nelson. They had bad timing at the wrong time."

Whatever the hell that meant. Desiree just shook her head and followed Bogarde, who started back up the street. When they reached his Ford, parked near Rampart, he called over the roof of the car, "We gotta lay out our plans."

He took her down Rampart Street and she noted the name of the street changed to St. Claude Avenue after they passed Elysian Fields Avenue. She'd noticed it that morning when she took the streetcar down the same neutral ground into St. Bernard Parish.

Bogarde parked in front of Rudy's Grill on St. Claude and she followed him into a typical diner, a counter on one side with a grill beyond, a line of booths on the other side, all up against the window facing the avenue, cash register up by the front door. The booths featured turquoise Formica table tops. There was a heavy set waiter and a very thin waitress with tired eyes and a jowly face to go along with her graying hair.

"Great burgers here," Bogarde said.

Desiree ordered the club sandwich and ginger ale.

"What? No coffee?" Bogarde asked after he ordered a burger, heavy on the mayo, extra French fries and coffee.

"OK." Bogarde leaned forward and lowered his voice. "The jewelry store. I think we should do it Friday at lunch time. A brazen daylight robbery." He leaned back to let the waitress deposit the coffee and ginger ale.

"I got a license plate from one of the used cars. I'll put it on the Ford, then take it off back at the lot. I'll pick you up at the corner of St. Ann and Dauphine. It's never busy there and we'll drive straight down to Chartres, hang left then a quick right a half block later. I been checking Madison Street and it's always got parking open."

His eyes danced as he went on. "We go straight in. You put on dark sunglasses and I'll put on the gorilla mask. We take all the money, all the loose gem stones and some of the jewelry and get out fast. We'll go down Decatur and hang a quick right."

The scent of Bogarde's burger on the grill filled the place. The door chimed behind them and two men in sweaty t-shirts and dungarees came in. Both checked out Desiree on their way to sit at the counter.

Bogarde lowered his voice even more. "In a getaway, you take as many right turns as you can. You turn left, you gotta wait for traffic to pass."

As if she was interested. Desiree had only driven a few times in her life and usually had problems with the damn gear shifts.

The waitress brought the club sandwich and her small serving of fries and came right back with Bogarde's food. He gobbled a couple fries right away, then went on. "I'll drop you off at Canal and Rampart and you can catch the streetcar back home. I'll be back at work before my lunch hour's over."

Desiree took a bite of the club sandwich. The bacon was crispy at least and the bread fresh. Bogarde wiped the mayonnaise that oozed from his mouth as he chewed a big chuck of his burger.

She noticed the men were watching her now, sizing her up and sizing up Bogarde who didn't even notice them. She felt her nerves start up, then reached down and patted her purse with the Detective Special inside. Ignoring the men, she finished off her sandwich but didn't touch the fries, which Bogarde downed after he'd finished his.

The waitress re-filled their drinks and Bogarde asked for the check. He left a fifty cent tip and Desiree added a dollar as she climbed out of the booth. The men let Bogarde pass but both stood up to block Desiree's path. She stopped short, blew a strand of loose hair and said, "You smell."

"You smell too, little lady." The second man turned to see what Bogarde would do and dropped his jaw as Bogarde cocked the forty-five pointed between the man's eyes.

"Uh ..." The man tried backing away but bumped against his friend who snarled, "What the fuck," until he saw the forty-five and froze.

"Excuse me," Desiree said as she slipped by them, looking at Bogarde's face. He talked a good game, her boyfriend, and she figured he was a wimp deep down inside. Maybe he was, but that big gun gave him a confidence she'd seen only once before, with Elmer, the mark from Topeka.

Bogarde stood there holding the gun in his right hand and the hand never wavered. He said nothing and didn't squint his eyes or try to look mean. Worse. He looked as if he felt nothing and she found herself putting a hand on his waist.

"Come on," she said. "They get the hint."

The two men inched backward, both with their hands up now. Desiree saw the waitress had a phone in her hand just as the woman said, "Police? There's a stick up at Rudy's Grill. Man with a big gun."

Bogarde looked at the waitress for a long moment, looked back at the two men and went, "Bam!"

The men fell back a step and Bogarde led the way out to the Ford, which was parked just up St. Claude. They jumped in and pulled away. Past Elysian Fields, they spotted a prowl car, red light blinking as it zoomed by on the way to Rudy's.

Bogarde found a spot right in front of Desiree's place, parked the Ford but didn't turn off the engine. His knuckles were white as he gripped the steering wheel.

"You're not coming up?"

"No." He looked straight out the windshield. "We gotta stay focused. Run the plan over in your mind again and again until it's second nature. I'll call you tomorrow night."

Desiree got out slowly and the Ford drove off. Her hand on her hip she watched the car make the corner and thought … weird as hell. She was juiced from the grill, felt the tingles and he just drove off.

Upstairs in her room as she undressed and let the day's work creep back in to let her know she was tired after all, she was glad he hadn't come up. She needed a night off. She opened her balcony doors and stepped out. The air was almost cool now and the courtyard below so dark she couldn't make out anything. A small noise turned her to the right and she spotted a black cat with yellow eyes looking down at her from the neighbor's rooftop.

"Here kitty," she said softly but the cat turned and walked away slowly.

Tomorrow she would shoot the Detective Special, made by Colt, carried by plainclothes cops and private detectives all over the world, as Mr. Clavin had explained. And at least one gun-moll.

•••

Jim's foot picked a bad time to act up and trying to work out the kinks only made it worse. It was so bad, he had to stop three times before he got to the newsstand and three more times before he climbed onto the stool at Morning Call. He'd taken four aspirins, but all they did was clear his head so he felt every piercing stab of pain.

It took a few minutes sitting on the stool for the throbbing to stop and a cup of black coffee, with all the sugar he added, to snap him out of the haze enough to open the *Santa Fe Pueblo* to the local news section where the drawing of the aliens was on page one.

They looked like naked scarecrows, thin arms and boney legs with a towel draped across their mid-section as they lay, belly-up, on what looked like an autopsy table. They weren't in pieces, however. Probably all males, just like American military pilots. Except, Jim remembered, for the women pilots who'd ferried planes from the U.S. to Britain during the war. He'd actual met one in the hospital after his foot was mangled. She'd been shot down over Ireland by a rogue Messerschmitt 109 on a suicide mission.

The heads of the aliens were almond shaped, pointy-headed with slanted, almond-shaped eyes almost too big for their heads.

The nose and mouth were small and the ears rounded. There was no hair indicated and their feet looked almost webbed in the drawing. The caption below the drawing read: *Described to our sketch artist by two eye-witnesses, this artist rendering is an accurate portrayal of the pilots of the craft that fell at the Foster Ranch outside Roswell, New Mexico, on or about July 4th*.

The article accompanying the drawing featured an interview with a soldier who preferred not to be named, a soldier from the Air-Force 509th Intelligence Office who had accompanied Major Jesse Marcel to the crash site. The 'super-strength' metallic material gathered at the sight could not be associated with anything of terrestrial origin and certainly not anything associated with a 'weather balloon' which is light weight. "This stuff was heavy. It took three men to pick up the largest piece and it was only a few feet in diameter."

The metal was of such a great sheen that it seemed to shimmer in different colors from battleship gray to shades purple, pink, blue and green, depending on how it was turned to the sunlight.

The story went on to elaborate how the U.S. Air Force's story that the debris was from a weather balloon simply defied logic, clashed with eye-witness accounts and did not seem plausible or even logical. One point that really stood out was the Air Force used nine trucks to haul away one aluminum foil and balsa wood balloon crushed to pieces.

The autopsy was described again, with two new revelations. The aliens had double eye-lids, one sheer, one opaque and they had what appeared to be a gastric mill, somewhat like a chicken's gizzard to go along with their glandular stomach. The interior wall of the alien gizzard was lined with cartilage-like plates which probably assisted in grinding the food which would pass back and forth to the stomach.

The 'gouge' created by the crash at the Foster Ranch, extended four or five hundred feet and was two to three feet deep. The article went on to hint of a second crash site at nearby Socorro, New Mexico.

Jim started up a second cup of coffee and re-read the article carefully. He had to admit, the stories in *Amazing, Astounding* and

Startling Stories were much better written and much more dramatic, but this was *real*.

• • •

By the time Desiree walked into Morning Call, Jim had just finished his fourth cup of coffee and a story from the latest edition of *Planet Stories* – a story set on a sun-kissed planet along the backwash of the Milky Way, a planet newly discovered by human explorers, a planet filled with creatures amazingly similar to Earth's dinosaurs.

Desiree's hair was fluffed out with no hairpins, looked freshly washed and even paler than usual. She wore a yellow sundress and low heels and carried a large black purse and a wide-brimmed hat in her left hand.

"Coffee? Beignets?"

"Nope. Had three cups today. Sorry I'm late. Dropped by the post office." Desiree had bought another money order to send home to her folks. This one was for a hundred bucks. More of the money she'd made from the Schroeder photos, like the money she'd paid for the Detective Special. She sent the money orders with no return address. Of course, it had a New Orleans postmark, but the chances of her folks coming to New Orleans was slim and no way they'd find her without a return address.

"You ready?"

He was about to tell her she was dressed wrong. They were going to shoot guns in the woods, but the thought of her in a dress, rather than dungarees, like him, was a far better sight. He tucked the newspaper and magazine into a carrying bag and followed her out.

"Did you bring a gun?" she asked.

He lifted the bag. Inside was the nine-millimeter Luger he'd taken off a grenadier he'd killed in the Hürtgen. Also inside was a hundred-round box of fresh ammo.

Desiree put the hat on and said, "I figured we'd be in the sun."

"The woods too. Or marsh."

He caught a whiff of her light perfume in the breeze.

"Maybe you should change into slacks," he heard himself say.

"Naw." She took his hand as they crossed at the foot of Esplanade. "If it gets sloppy I can take off the dress."

He took in a deep breath and she laughed one of those deep, sexy, throaty laughs.

They caught the Elysian Fields streetcar up to Gentilly Boulevard and the bus all the way to the end of the line. Desiree wouldn't let Jim pay her fare. Sitting next to him, their legs up against each other in the narrow seats, they both looked out at the occasional bar and grocery store as they moved from subdivisions of small brick homes to other subdivisions and eventually there was only woods, marshland on either side of the road which was now Highway 90. Desiree recognized the route they'd taken with Elmer, glanced at that last Esso where Bogarde had hidden in the men's room before coming out in that silly mask to hide in the trunk.

At the end of the line, when the bus turned around before crossing The Rigolets bridge, Desiree and Jim were the only two passengers left and departed. The driver gave them a sideward glance as they stepped down.

There were several fishing camps up on pilings along the Lake Catherine side of the road, all behind small fences. Jim told her it was actually Lake Saint Catherine on the map, but it was one of those New Orleans things, like calling Burgundy Street – Bur*gun*dy and Milan Street – *My*lin and medians – neutral grounds.

Jim led her across the highway to the side away from the lake and nodded ahead. "Go far enough up there and you're in Lake Pontchartrain." He waved his arm as they moved into the woods, walking carefully now on a slight ridge that grew higher away from the road. "This area is called Bayou Sauvage. It's the biggest swamp within the city limits of an American city. It's huge."

A few steps later and the heat washed over from them as the land on either side of the ridge became a cypress swamp. It was like walking through a steam bath, the air heavy and thick, the heat shimmering on the green-brown swamp water. At least the hat kept the sun off Desiree's head, but even in the shade of the tallest oaks and cypress she'd ever seen, it was flat-out hot.

"I wonder what 'Sauvage' means? Savage?"

"It's French. Means wild or untamed."

Thankfully, Jim stopped beneath a wide oak tree and pointed to part of an old wooden fence that had been partially consumed by the swamp. Desiree looked back and couldn't see the highway anymore. No way she could hear any cars with the sound of the cicadas rising and falling, along with the sound of buzzing insects that sounded like dive-bombers in a war flick.

At that moment she saw the first spider hanging on a tremendous web from an oak branch. A black and gold, fierce-looking spider, nearly three inches in diameter, moved slowly along its web, its long legs flexing, showing off the black tuffs of hair at its leg joints.

"Silk spider," Jim said, moving close to her. "They won't bother you."

"They're already bothering me."

She took a few steps back along the ridge and noticed, looking around more carefully, there were more silk spiders in the tree. She looked at the ground. At least up on the ridge they would see any cottonmouths before the bastard could sneak up on them and a gator would have to climb up a ways to get to them.

Jim put his bag down.

"Is that a German Luger?" Desiree dug her Detective Special from her purse.

"Yes. You know Lugers?"

"Saw it in the movies, silly. Major Strasser pulled one just before Rick plugged him at the airport."

Casablanca. Oh, yeah, thought Jim, as he slipped a loaded magazine into the Luger and chambered a round. He slipped the Luger into his waistband and held out his hand.

"Yours first."

She handed him the Colt and he opened the cylinder, dropped the six rounds into his left palm and then closed the cylinder. He aimed at the fence and squeezed the trigger.

"Nice even action. Not too loose. Not too tight." He handed the gun back to Desiree. "You've been dry-firing it?"

She shrugged. "Not enough." She aimed at the fence with the gun in her right hand and pulled the trigger. It was a little hard, but not too much and the gun felt nice and heavy in her palm. She grabbed her right wrist with her left hand and pulled the trigger again as she aimed.

Jim slipped her bullets into his pocket and held his hand out for her gun again. He took it in his right hand and wrapped his left hand around the other side of the grip.

"Two handed position. It's what they taught us in the army and what cops do." He showed her how his hands were wrapped around the butt of the gun. "Extend your arms straight out, look at the front sight through the rear sights and squeeze the trigger." He closed his left eye and aimed and dry-fired the Colt before passing it to her.

He arranged her fingers and it felt natural when they were aligned and wrapped together the gun, now cupped in the palm of her left hand as well. She squeezed the trigger three more times, slowly, watching the hammer pull back then fall forward.

Jim handed her the six rounds again and she loaded the Colt.

"Aim at one of the fence slats," he said. He put the palms of his hand together. "And push against either side of the gun with both hands as you aim. It'll steady you."

He was right. Desiree aimed carefully and pulled the trigger slowly and when the hammer fell it almost made her jump. It was louder than she'd thought.

"Dead on," he said as they both stared at the neat hole in the center of the slat, up top, just where Desiree was aiming. "That was perfect. It's supposed to surprise you when it goes off."

She fired the remaining five and but missed the slat twice.

"Not bad," Jim said. "You rushed the two you missed."

She wiped perspiration from her forehead and reloaded. Jim took out the Luger and aimed at the next slat along the fence. He fired the first two slowly and increased the pace until he'd emptied the magazine. The Luger's report was sharper than the Colt's.

"It's a nine millimeter," explained Jim. "If you got plus-p rounds, yours would be even louder."

Desiree shielded her eyes from the sun and looked at his slat. "You're just showing off."

"Nope. I missed one. Only seven holes over there." He turned around and pointed to another rickety fence on the other side of the ridge. Their backs were to the sun now and Desiree didn't have to shield her eyes. She hit her slat with all six rounds this time. He hit the one next to hers with his eight rounds.

In the insufferable heat, the sharp smell of the gunpowder seemed so thick, Desiree struggled to breathe. Jim had them walk another twenty yards down the fence line. He had her shoot three quick shots, pause, then three quick shots again. He let her shoot the Luger which was heavier but had less recoil and seemed to be smoother to shoot.

She didn't realize how hot the barrel became until she almost touched it and realized. They moved back toward the road, stopping to shoot at a log in the brackish water, then at some lily pads.

As she reloaded again, Jim stepped around her and fired again and she looked up to see a large black snake coil into a ball as Jim's bullets struck it. The snake fell off the log into the water and Jim said, "Cottonmouth."

Desiree noticed the spiders again as they got closer to the roadway. A cloud moved in front of the sun and it dimmed a few minutes. Jim pointed behind them at some angry-looking gray clouds.

"They're coming off Pontchartrain," he said. "We're about to get wet."

They made it back to the highway, their guns tucked back in the bags, before the rain came. Fat drops plopped around them and then on them, isolated drops, like fallout from a distant rainstorm. Then the rainstorm was no longer distant and the fat drops pelted them, washed over them, hammered them.

Jim opened his mouth to the cool rain and laughed.

Desiree laughed too and shouted, "When does the bus come?"

"You got me."

Chapter 8
YOU HAVE A RADIO, DON'T YOU

By the time a big red and white Buick stopped and the driver, a man with slick-black hair, leaned over and rolled down the front passenger window, Desiree and Jim were drenched and the rain was still pelting them.

"You kids get in the back seat," the driver said and Desiree thought the guy looked familiar. She climbed in first and Jim followed, shutting the door quickly.

"You play tenor sax at the 500 Club, right?" said Jim.

"Bingo. Louis Prima's band," the driver said as they pulled away.

"Morning Call," Desiree said, remembering where they'd seen the guy the other day. She ran her hands down her arms to shed the rain on the floorboard. "We're getting your car soaked."

The driver laughed loudly and gunned the accelerator but only for a few seconds, letting up and slowing down the big car.

"It'll dry," he said, then glanced back at Desiree with grin. "I still think you're too good for Hotsy Jazz." He turned back to the road. "Even with your make-up running."

Desiree wrung her hair, letting it drip on the floorboard.

"I'm Sam," said the man.

"I'm Jim and you know Miss Desiree Blanc."

Sam grinned at her again, this time in the rear view mirror. "Miss Desiree Raccoon, you mean."

Desiree let out a long sigh and dug her compact from her purse. Yep. Her eye-liner had run, surrounding her eyes in a black raccoon ring. A flash of lightning was instantly followed by a loud slap of thunder and the car actually shuddered. The rain increased so much it was almost impossible to see out of the car, but Sam managed to keep the Buick on the road. He slowed down as they eased into the city, passing the motels and barrooms on the outskirts until they reached the city proper along Gentilly.

The rain slammed against the Buick in waves, then finally settled into a heavy downpour when the wind quit rocking the car.

"Bet it doesn't rain like this where y'all are from," Sam finally broke the silent drive.

Jim shook his head and Desiree said, "I've never seen it this bad."

"With that accent, you gotta be from Mississippi," he told Desiree. "I'm headin' back from a gig in Bay St. Louis." Sam laughed as another wave slashed against the windshield, as if a giant bucket of water had been tossed at them. "One day, we'll all wash away. Y'all know we're living in the largest American city under sea level?"

Lightning stuck a telephone pole a half block up and Sam turned the Buick immediately and took a side street.

"Jesus," Jim said. Desiree took his hand and squeezed.

The Buick made its way toward the Quarter and Jim held Desiree's hand and wondered how in the hell could his heart race by just holding hands. Elysian Fields was flooded and the Buick seemed to float into the St. Claude intersection. Sam stopped in the middle of the neutral round where the streetcar tracks were somewhat raised.

"Where do y'all live anyway? I got take a left soon. Live in Bywater, funny name, huh?

"I'm on Frenchmen," said Desiree. "Are we close?"

"I'm on Marigny. Might be a little closer."

"Well, its probably not as deep down Elysian. The city's higher near the river." Sam gunned the Buick and they sailed through the intersection, the Buick making waves as it moved. Desiree watched the waves roll to the banquettes and up against the front stoops of the raised buildings.

"Chartres never floods," Sam said with obvious relief when he turned off the avenue on to one-way Chartres Street.

"I'm a block up," said Jim when they reached Marigny Street.

"OK." Sam stopped.

Jim led the way, helping Desiree up on the banquette. They moved through ankle deep water as the Buick edged away. By the time they started up the front stoop of Jim's Creole Cottage, the water was half-way up their calves.

They stood dripping just inside the doorway for a moment before Jim bolted across the small living room and into the bathroom. He brought out two large towels, passed one to Desiree before going back into the bathroom to light the gas heater in the wall. It was a new device, made of white ceramic and he started up a warm bath, but not too warm.

Desiree was running the towel through her hair.

"You're shivering," he said.

"I know."

He took her hand and led her into the bathroom, then backed out. "There's a robe hanging behind the door."

• • •

The warm bath was perfect but Desiree turned off the heater as soon as she climbed out and opened the frosted window to let in some cooler air. The rain had let up but it was still drizzling. It was a man's robe, plaid, but not too short.

Jim was sitting on the floor, his Luger in pieces on the coffee table in front of him. He had on a white T-shirt that looked brand new and gray shorts, a gray sock on his left foot, probably to cover the scar.

"Well, this is what I look like without make-up."

He smiled. "You look fine. More than fine." He started to get up. "They teach you how to clean your weapon when you bought it?"

"No." She sat on the sofa.

Jim got up a little gingerly and limped away. "I've got coffee and muffins in the kitchen."

"Muffins?"

He shrugged. "My landlady makes them every day and leaves some for me. These look like carrot cake."

Mrs. O'Keefe was serious about her muffins and these were quite tasty, maybe too sweet but they went well with the strong coffee. As they munched, Jim showed her how to clean the Colt, which should be done after each firing.

"I was thinking of asking you to a movie tonight," Jim said as he wiped the excess oil from her revolver. "At the Joy Theater. Movie called *The Long Night* with Henry Fonda and Vincent Price. The paper said it was about a WWII veteran who kills a con man." He gave her that sly smile. "Didn't count on a flood of biblical proportions."

"You have a radio, don't you?"

They were on the sofa now, at either end, empty coffee cups and crumbled muffin wrappers next to the cleaned guns on the coffee tables.

"I have a radio."

"We could dance." As soon as she said it, her eyes went wide. "I'm sorry."

Jim laughed as he got up. "So you've seen me dance."

"No. I … um."

He turned on the Philco radio and rotated the dial until he found 'Moonlight Serenade' just starting. Jim turned and held out a hand. "I can slow dance."

She moved to him and he took her in his arms, moving gently with the music. She felt every inch of her body as she pressed against him, as if every nerve wanted to get in on the action. He cupped his left hand around her right and pressed his right hand against her lower back as they glided slowly, sensuously in the small living room.

It was weird how well they fit so well together, her face pressed against his neck. Maybe it was the weather. Maybe it was the excitement from all that shooting or the calming bath that made her feel as she was floating, as if both were floating. As the song ended, Desiree looked up at Jim and his mouth moved down to hers, just like in the movies, in slow motion, and the kiss was feathery soft, scintillating and thrilling at the same moment and that was before the tongues went to work.

They left the robe on the floor just outside the bedroom and she helped him out of the T-shirt, shorts and jockeys. "I hope you have a rubber," she gasped.

He nodded and reached for the small table next to his bed.

Jim looked at Desiree as she climbed on the bed and lay there on her back. The light from the living room streamed across her naked body and her skin seemed to glow white hot. She wasn't smiling, but there was a knowing look on her face, a ready look. For a moment Jim felt as if he'd slipped into a story from *Amazing* or *Astounding,* because the impossible was about to happen.

His hands shook when he ran his fingers through his hair, pulling the hair from his eyes but he wasn't as nervous as he thought he would be and moved to kiss her belly and up to those perfectly symmetrical breasts. Jim tried to take his time making love to this woman but she wanted no part of that and it was frenzied and wild. They knocked the lamp off the side table and he was sure the pictures on the wall were hanging crooked after, as they lay on the bed, damp with perspiration.

He got up to lose the rubber and grabbed two cold beers from his small fridge. Stella Artois beer and it went down smooth.

"I don't usually like beer, but this is more like champagne beer," said Desiree.

"It's Belgian."

Desiree looked at him. "The Battle of the Bulge was in Belgium, wasn't it?"

He nodded and took another hit of beer. She waited for him to say something, maybe about the battle or the war but he just lay there, propped up on a pillow and sipping the beer. She took another hit and he spoke to the ceiling in a low voice, "There was a worse battle, before the Bulge. The Hürtgen Forest. It was in Germany, right next to the Ruhr River. Conifer trees, they told me later. Dense forest, rough terrain and Jerry was dug in. Grenadiers mostly. My division, the First Infantry, the Big Red One, took a mauling but wouldn't give up. Americans don't give up."

Jim stared straight ahead, eyes unfocused. He leaned his head up to take another sip of beer before going on. "The shelling was the worst part. Krauts aimed over our heads, air bursts that shredded the trees and sent thousands of splinters down on us, some as big as a man's arm, razor sharp.

"After, to recuperate, they sent our division behind the lines, to another forest back in Belgium, the Ardennes, just where Hitler launched his attack. The Battle of the Bulge." Jim lifted his left foot with the sock still on it. "That's where I got this."

"You get any medals?"

"Purple heart and a bronze star."

She got up on an elbow. "Purple heart's for being wounded, that I know. But what's the bronze star for?"

"Heroic or meritorious achievement while engaged in an action against an enemy of the United States. In this case, the 1st

SS Panzer Division. We blew up a buncha their tanks. I was a sniper but I learned how to use a bazooka pretty well."

The next few seconds of quiet was broken by a horn blaring outside.

"I wasn't heroic at all," he said in a low, distant voice. "It was kill them before they killed us."

Sex the second time around took a lot longer and Desiree could see the affection in Jim's eyes as he looked down into hers. The rain started up again and a cool breeze came in through the window screens, blowing across their bodies as they lay side by side after. Desiree rarely fell asleep right after making love but her eye-lids were so heavy, she couldn't keep them open and she drifted away.

• • •

She woke to a sizzling sound and smelled bacon cooking. Desiree went out and peeked at the kitchen area to find Jim in his shorts and lone sock standing at a small stove. He turned and shrugged, "I got hungry."

"I'm famished." Desiree reached back for the robe and put it on. "What time is it, anyway?" It was pitch outside.

"Three-fifteen. How do you like your eggs?"

"Sunny side up."

The man made a good breakfast and as Desiree ate, she realized she was supposed to call Bogarde last night. He'd been setting up the jewelry store heist and was probably mad as hell. Well, he'd just have to be mad for a while.

"Since we're off today too, wanna go to that movie?" His eyes shined in the bright kitchen like, like dark brown agates.

"I have something to take care of around lunchtime, but sure, we'll take in a flick after."

"Good."

• • •

She called Bogarde from a pay phone before he left for work that morning. He started yelling immediately and would have taken off her head if she'd seen him in person. He called off the jewelry heist, broke up the 'beauty-and-the-beast gang', called her a no good bitch and what the hell was she doing last night, anyway.

"None of your business." She was about to hang up but he must have realized and said, "Be ready at noon sharp. St. Ann and Dauphine. Put a raincoat over your outfit." He hung up.

Although she knew she looked a mess in her wrinkled dress, no make-up and hair afly, she attracted the attention of several men as she walked the rest of the way home. One sweaty guy gave her a, "Hey Baby," when she passed but she ignored him. Men were such simpletons.

Later, soaking in her tub, she thought of Jim limping around his apartment, fixing her breakfast, smiling at her with that twinkle in his eyes. His eyes. They told her there was a lot of affection for her in that man. It's not good, she told herself. The last thing she needed was to fall in love. She was a gun-moll on her way to Hollywood. New Orleans was just as stopover and settling down with a replanted dustbowl Okie wasn't in her master plan. What worried her was her reactions when with Jim. It was so natural with him. Too natural.

Just before noon, Desiree Blanc stopped at the corner of St. Ann and Dauphine Streets and pretended to look at the magazines at the small newsstand outside Liuzza's Grocery Store. She had on a dark green rain coat over the teddy she'd wear into the jewelry store. Bogarde's idea, figuring the old men inside would see the sheer, black teddy, which hid little of her body, and not look anywhere else. He'd be in his gorilla mask and she would wear dark sunglasses so their faces wouldn't be exposed. She'd teased out her hair, put on plenty make-up, which drew the stares of the newspaper seller and every man she'd passed on her way to St. Ann and Dauphine. She should have put a bag over her head.

Shifting her purse from one shoulder to the other, she felt the heft of the freshly-cleaned Colt Detective Special. She couldn't wait to pull it out in the jewelry store. Bogarde's eyes might pop out.

Just as the bell of St. Louis Cathedral starting ringing, Bogarde pulled up. She resisted checking to make sure he'd switched the license plate. She climbed in. He gave her the once over and said, "Lose the rain coat," before heading down St. Ann. Just as he made the turn to Chartres Street, he hit the brakes.

A fire engine sat in middle of the narrow street, firemen hustling around it, two of them attaching a hose to a fire hydrant.

"Son of a bitch!" Bogarde tried backing up but he was blocked by a Studebaker.

Looking back, Desiree saw a prowl car pull up on the banquette behind the Studebaker and one of the cops moved back up St. Ann to clear the traffic. The other cop came their way and she tried to sink down in the seat, only her blond hair naturally attracted the cop's attention and he looked in at her. He stopped and looked at the teddy, smiled, then started laughing as he moved on toward the fire trucks.

"It's never busy here," she heard herself give Bogarde his words back as she pulled the rain coat back on but not before two firemen came over to check her out. They pretended like they were looking for another hydrant but one of them winked at her. She noticed two elderly men standing outside Roth's Jewelers as they watched the commotion in the street and the smoke coming from a small restaurant across Chartres. The men were almost identical, short, nearly completely bald. Both wore thick eye-glasses, black slacks, a white shirt and black tie.

"The Roth brothers?" she asked Bogarde when he noticed the two.

"Yeah. They're almost midgets." He put the car into reverse and followed the Studebaker backing up St. Ann. The cop directing traffic at St. Ann and Royal gave Desiree a look as they moved by, even though she had the raincoat closed.

Bogarde had to go up Royal. When he started to pull over Desiree snapped, "Drive me home."

"OK. OK. I don't wanna be late back to work, that's all."

"You won't be late."

Bogarde pounded the steering wheel. "It woulda worked."

"It'll still work. We just need to pick a day when there's no fire across the street."

He glared at her and the tension went right out of him. "Yeah."

"Coulda been worse," she said. "Fire could have started after we were inside, fire engine blocking your parked car. You imagine me running away in these heels in a see-through teddy?"

It wasn't until they were pulling up on Frenchmen Street that Bogarde said, "Where were you last night?"

She kissed her index finger and pressed it against Bogarde's lips. "A girl has to have some secrets, you know." She climbed out.

"You're such a goddamn smart-ass, sometimes," he snarled.

"Yeah. Well I hope the cops didn't see that gorilla mask on your back seat."

Bogarde closed his eyes, hit the gas and just left.

• • •

The Joy Theater smelled like new carpet. It just opened in February, with over twelve hundred seats. Ultra-modern, icy air-frigeration, a large balcony and even a 'crying room' for babies. Jim positioned them in the center at the front of the large balcony where no one could sit in front of them and they had a great view of the screen. Desiree cuddled against him in the almost chilly atmosphere.

The place was crowded on a Friday night and for some reason the Henry Fonda movie wasn't playing. Instead a dark film, *Out of the Past* with Robert Mitchum, Jane Greer, Kirk Douglas and Rhonda Fleming, was featured and it didn't take long for Desiree to know it was her kind of flick. The big, good looking lug, Robert Mitchum was fishing with his sweet, goody-two-shoes girlfriend, when he got a visitor who drew Mitchum – a former private detective – into a rendezvous with his past where a dame waited. A flashback showed the dame, Jane Greer, shooting four times at the big-shot gangster played with creepy charm by Kirk Douglas. She only hit him once, which drew a comment about a dame with a rod is like a guy with a knitting needle.

Desiree was sure if she'd fired four times, she'd hit something as big as Kirk Douglas four times.

Greer fled with forty grand and Mitchum was hired to catch her and bring her back. Kirk wanted the woman more than the money. Some dame. Mitchum tracked her to Acapulco and Desiree knew they would link up, had to link up, it was so damn dangerous they had to. Greer wasn't a great beauty by Hollywood standards but she drew the big lug to her like a black widow spider, an evil, sexy woman who'd do anything to get her way.

There were beach scenes and a sudden rainstorm. Jim squeezed Desiree's hand and she brushed his neck with her lips. And the two star-crossed lovers on the screen could not pull away from each other. For them there was no past and no future.

Of course, the gangster showed up and Greer and Mitchum barely escaped to live for a while in dark, secretive places. There was a double-cross when Mitchum's old partner showed up and wanted a cut of the money and Greer shot him, then cleverly abandoned Mitchum, which allowed him to find his new goody-two-shoes girlfriend. But he had to face his past.

"The man is doomed," Jim whispered.

Mitchum was seduced once again by wicked Greer and sucked into a complex web of intrigue, passion, betrayal, double and triple crosses and inevitable death. The movie had so many twists that Desiree couldn't believe there was yet another and another, even another dangerous woman, until the riveting climax where the doomed lovers died.

"Jesus, that was intense," she said as they walked out into the early evening heat.

"How about supper?" Jim asked.

Desiree swung her arms with Jim's hand in hers and felt like a high-schooler walking down Canal Street. "What do you have in mind?"

"I don't know. We could try Acme Oyster House. Great seafood."

She poked his ribs. "You're gonna needs some oysters, mister."

•••

Bogarde lay on the dry side of the double bed, Fanny Depardieu lightly snoring next to him, her dark brown hair half-covering her face. Bogarde looked at the three new suits Fanny had surprised him with earlier. They hung side by side outside her closet. Nicely tailored suits, Hart, Schaffner & Marx from Rubenstein Brothers. When he tried them on he found a crisp hundred dollar bill in the inside pocket of each coat.

"You look dreamy in good clothes," Fanny said as she helped him in and out of the suits. And, to think, he'd almost stood her up that evening, wanting to talk over the day's near disaster with

Desiree, but Desiree wasn't home so he dropped in on Chippy Number Two and viola, Fanny presented him with the suits.

She also presented him with a proposition. Quit Z Best Cars and open his own lot. She'd inherited several properties around town and one was being used as a parking lot on Tulane Avenue, not far from Charity Hospital, an ideal location, even better than Z Best's location on Canal because there were too many residences along Canal and Tulane was all business.

"You can get away from that awful man," she'd said, meaning Jiminy, of course. She had to drop by, right after lunch, to talk with Bogarde because Jiminy wouldn't put her calls through. Bogarde, flushed from the fiasco on Chartres Street, had just gotten back to Z Best when Fanny pulled up in her '47 black Cadillac convertible with its red interior, white wall tires, flared fenders and oversized chrome grill. She waved Bogarde over and asked him to drop by that evening. Jiminy came rushing over, salivating at the prospect that this woman might want to sell a brand new car and immediately disappointed when Fanny gave him the brush off.

Now, in bed, looking up at the ceiling, Bogarde let his mind wander for a moment to owning his own car lot. No way he was giving up the 'beauty-and-the-beast gang' at the moment, but the car lot would be a wonderful front and could give him access to a number of get-a-way cars.

Yeah. Maybe he should take up the widow Depardieu.

• • •

When Jim dropped off the magazines Leo had loaned him, Leo held up the latest *Santa Fe Pueblo* and said, "D'you read this story?"

He had. There was a picture of a weather balloon and an army colonel accompanying an article with an elaborate explanation of the Air Force's weather balloon story. They were high altitude balloons, launched from Alamogordo at night, flown across the New Mexican skies, some landing as far away as west Texas, others ending up in Arizona, Utah and Colorado.

"They sure came up with a detailed account," said Leo. "It's a cover story. Had it ready before the crash, I'll bet."

The men went into Leo's kitchen for a beer before going to work. Jim had drunk so much coffee that Saturday after his second night with Desiree. He had to force himself to not call her, not go by her place, not think of her, only that he couldn't do. He took a nap in the middle of the day and it helped. His foot wasn't aching as much today and he laughed at himself, wondering if that was all he needed. Plenty of sex.

"So, how are you and blondie getting along?"

Jim paused, Miller High Life half raised to his mouth.

"Saw y'all yesterday, coming out of the Joy like a couple teenagers, all googly-eyed. Didn't see me, didja?"

Jim shook his head and took a hit of beer.

"Maybe her boyfriend saw you too."

That struck Jim in the belly. "I wish he did."

"Yeah," Leo agreed. "I'd like to see you snap him like a pretzel."

A sly grin came to Leo's face, reminding Jim of the way Clark Gable looked when he was about to zing someone. "So, how's it feel to be the other man? To be Jody?"

Jim took another hit as the cadence came back to him, the old army marching rhyme, step by step. "You hadda get home with your *left,*" called out the sergeant as they stepped with their left foot. "You're *right,*" the men responded as the right foot fell. "You hadda get home with your *left*. You're *right*. Your baby was *there* when you *left*. You're *right*. Jody was *there* when you *left*. You're *right*. Sound *off*. One, *two*. Sound *off*. Three, *four*. Cadence *count*. One, *two*, three, *four*. One, *two*. Three *four*."

Yeah, Jody. The man putting the moves on your baby while you're in combat. Probably a four-f'er, draft dodger, malingerer and Jim was sure that fit this Bogarde fella to a fuckin' tee. Son-of-a-bitch never saw combat. You could see it in his eyes.

"I'm not Jody," Jim said. "He's Jody."

"That's what I meant. Only he got there first."

"It's last that counts, ain't it?"

Leo nodded and they sat there for a while. Jim could see Leo wasn't finished.

Leo finally said, "We Americans treat our women too well. In the old country, the women listened, weren't no women voting, they knew their place. They're almost equals here."

"What old country?"

"Take your pick."

"Yeah, they got it made here," Jim chuckled. "Can take off their clothes for money."

"What? Yeah."

"Is this a great country or what?"

Chapter 9

TELL ME YOU DIDN'T LEAVE YOUR GUN BEHIND

Working Sunday evening was never fun. The crowds at Hotsy Jazz were small and the men more raucous, yelling comments until one of Baddie's men eased over to quiet them. Desiree didn't look forward to it. She'd set up an appointment with Dennis Schroeder to pick up the nudes at two p.m., so she'd have time to bring them back home before getting to work at four.

It was sizzling out and thick rain clouds threatened overhead as she rang the doorbell at 725 Royal Street, which Schroeder answered immediately. He wore another untucked white shirt, this time over khaki pants and looked around as he let her in.

"You're alone?"

"You disappointed?"

"Oh, no. I … um … just thought Mr. Badalamente."

She went up the stairs, "I'm a big girl, Schroeder. I go out by myself sometimes." She felt the reassuring weight of the Detective Special in her purse.

Desiree didn't know what she'd expected, but she didn't expect the photos to look *that* good. They didn't even look like her. Well, they were her but they were … gorgeous. The light, her skin like satin, the shadows and the dark spaces as black as pitch. Her lips glistened with what looked like an artificial wetness.

"It's the red lipstick. On black and white film, red is as black as it gets."

The outdoor shots were completely different, softer, less sexy and she looked radiant in the sunlight.

"Did you touch these up?" she asked.

"Slightly, but not much at all. Your hair is such a luscious color, it was easy."

There were several close-ups of her face, one in particular, a half profile, made her almost gasp. "It looks like a Hollywood promotional picture."

"You'd light up the screen, young lady."

She looked at Schroeder and the shy look he returned told her he was being honest and wasn't on the make in the least.

"How can I get copies of these?"

"These are your copies."

"All of them?"

"Everyone. When I tell you you're worth it, you're *worth* it. I'll make a lot of money from these in Europe. Full front nudes of a woman as exotic as you ..." his voice trailed off.

"Brunettes are exotic, blonds are icy," she said.

"Then you're icy exotic."

She laughed as he started packing the photos into a cardboard box for her.

"These are eight by ten inches and five by sevens. They fit standard frames."

She leaned over and kissed him on the cheek and he seemed surprised. He cleared his throat and said, "I'd like to shoot you again."

"Why not?"

"Well." He looked down at his feet for a second. "Would you consider posing with another model?"

"What kind of posing?"

He shook his head. "No touching. Nothing like that. Just two naked bodies posing side by side. Sitting, standing, lying down, but no touching. I'm not talking about sex shots."

"OK. What does she look like?"

"A man," he said and took a hesitant step back.

"Pose naked with a naked man?"

Schroeder nodded, his eyes wide in anticipation of a negative answer. He cleared his throat and said, "A naked man with skin so black it looks blue."

It was her turn to take a hesitant step back, a hand moving to her hip.

"Five hundred dollars for two hours," Schroeder spoke quickly. "He's a nice man. A minister. He modeled before and now he's reaching thirty and he's heard about you, and ..."

"Heard?" Desiree looked at the box and said, "Did you show him my pictures?"

"No."

She knew he was fibbing now. He had to be showing these shots around.

"The contrast of your skin and his dark skin would be so dramatic."

"And I'll bet they'll sell very well in Europe."

Schroeder shrugged and said, "Oh my, yes. Especially in West Germany, Austria, Scandinavia."

"Does he get five hundred too?"

"Oh, no, he's paying just for the honor of posing with you. He'll get copies of course, but he can't show them around, not being a minister. You know what'd happened with his congregation if they found out."

"Not to mention his wife."

"Yes," Schroeder nodded. "He's a happily married man. A good Christian ..."

"Who wants to pose naked with a Bourbon Street stripper."

Schroeder seemed a little relieved. "Not just any stripper, but the blond desire herself. Desiree Blanc."

She thought about it a minute and Schroeder waited patiently.

"You don't have to decide now."

For a moment she saw the smiling face of the large Negro she's passed the other day, the man hosing down the street and checking her out as she passed. Then she recalled the wide-eyes of the man she flashed behind Hotsy Jazz when she'd stepped into the courtyard behind Hotsy after putting on her make-up. She had on a g-string and high heels, the man working on a brick wall who stood half-hidden by a tree as he watched her. She'd pretended she didn't see him.

She remembered the way she raised her arms, put her hands behind her head, closed her eyes and felt the man's eyes on her. Her heart raced and she was so turned on by it she dragged Bogarde to his apartment after and attacked him.

"Signore Badalamente's man has to come along."

"Most assuredly." Schroeder agreed.

"Then set it up and call me." Desiree picked a pencil from the drawing table and jotted the number to her boarding house on the table.

Schroeder thanked her again and said he'd set up the shoot.

By the time she reached the street, Desiree was having second thoughts, but only for a few moments. She laughed. She was paid to take off her clothes almost every night. Five hundred for two hours work, naked or not, was something she wasn't about to pass up. With Turtle there, there'd be no double cross, no grabbing or anything like that, she was sure.

Desiree hurried home to put the nudes away. She kept the cash in her purse, which would be safer in the dressing room than at home. None of the girls would steal from each other and woe-betide the fool who would steal anything from anyone who worked at Hotsy Jazz.

• • •

Later, in the dressing room as she put the finishing touches on her make-up, contouring those lips, Desiree figured the only way to work this was to see Jim before she went to work at four, when Bogarde was at work, and see Bogarde after she got off, the nights he bothered to come by. She'd talk to Jim about it when she got off unless Bogarde was waiting. If so, she'd talk to Jim tomorrow. She'd talked to neither during that day and it was nice having most of Sunday off before starting the work week.

The last two nights with Jim were incredibly sexy and he was a much more attentive lover than Bogarde, but they were the 'beauty-and-the-beast gang' and there were some good payoffs in the future. She reminded herself she needed to go to her bank soon as she stood and checked herself out in the full-length mirror.

Yes, that was the only way to work it with two men in her life. The only way.

• • •

To Desiree's surprise it worked just like that. She told Jim she had to do it that way until she figured out what to do with her life. She told herself she couldn't have sex every night with these two, so she slowed that part down, only with Jim it was hard, very hard to keep away from that with him. The only problem was in Jim's eyes when she left Hotsy Jazz with Bogarde, Sunday and Monday night. He looked hurt but gritted it out and never mentioned it when she saw him the following day.

It was Tuesday evening when Desiree spotted a familiar, grinning face in the crowd. Thomas, alias Tennessee, from Pirate Alley sat right up against the stage with a tall, blond man in a white suit. Thomas wore baby blue seersucker and a straw hat that

Turtle make him take off as Desiree started her act. She added a little something to the show, focusing on Thomas, but as she watched his reaction and that of his friend, she realized they were more interested in each other than her but that was OK. They might touch each other's hand discreetly, but they watched her moves and threw bills at her and clapped the loudest.

Between numbers, she actually went out to be with them. When she came out, Thomas was still there but his friend had left. She glanced at the bar but Jim wasn't in yet. She went over and Thomas got up and bowed as she sat.

"You have a way, young lady. Poetry in slow motion."

"How's the novel going?"

"Play, my dearest. I'm a playwright."

Of course. "That other guy. Faulkner. He wrote novels, right?" She shrugged.

"A sort of novel," Thomas said, "with sentences as long as the big muddy Mississippi."

Leo sent a club soda to her via a waitress and Thomas bubbled over Desiree, telling her he'd loved her incandescence, her vitality, her sheer blondness.

"I'll use you in a play, my dear. You may not recognize yourself. You may even be a man, but I'll drop pieces of you in some characters who sorely need pieces of you." The man's chubby face was radiant with joy and he was such a pleasure to listen to.

• • •

On Wednesday night, she spotted James Gallagher of the Chartres National Bank sitting in the crowd with his fake moustache. It was the first she'd seen of him since the restaurant. She made sure to make eye-contact with him as she danced and took off her panties right in front of him.

In the dressing room, after her last show, she changed quickly, hurrying to go and sidle up to Gallagher. She was putting the finishing contours to her lipstick when …

"This boyfriend 'a yours," said a deep, gravelly voice.

Desiree jumped at its suddenness.

Alphonso Badalamente stepped out of the dark corner. "I'm not talkin' about your bar-back boyfriend. I'm talkin' about your dandy boyfriend."

Desiree's throat was too tight for her to say anything. She felt her heart beating rapidly.

"He's up to something." Baddie leaned against the door frame. "I don't expect you to tell me but I'm tellin' you to tell him to stop. Capiche?"

She just stared into the dark, unblinking eyes.

"Capiche?"

She nodded.

He kept staring into her eyes as he said, "There's little that goes on in this city we don't know about."

She nodded again.

"If I have to talk to him," Baddie went on, "he'll probably say something stupid back and I'll have to hurt him."

She was still nodding.

"Schroeder tells me you're posing again. We set it up for next Saturday, the twenty-sixth. Turtle will meet you outside the studio at noon."

The stare continued for a full minute before Baddie backed out of the room. Desiree took in a deep breath and sat there thinking about it as came Toni Two-Lane rushed in, grumbling about being kept out of the room. When Desiree went out, Gallagher wasn't there. Bogarde was, waiting by the bar. Jim pretending not to notice him as he washed glasses, arms wet up to his elbows.

She went up to Bogarde and whispered in his ear, "Gallagher was here a few minutes ago."

Bogarde got off the stool. "Where?"

Desiree looked around. "He's gone now."

She took his hand and pulled him toward the door. "We gotta talk," she said. Over her shoulder her eyes met Jims and she tried a weak smile. They blew through a cloud of cigar smoke from the two bouncers standing outside the door and were half-way down the block when Desiree told him, "We have a worse problem."

"Dammit. Did you flirt with him at least?"

"Who?" She had to dodge two drunken sailors, stepping into the street momentarily.

"Who?" Bogarde snapped, "Gallagher!"

"No. Yes. I took my panties off for him."

Bogarde stopped, which made her stop. "Did you talk to him?"

She put a fist against her hip. "Did you see him when you came in?"

"No."

"I came out after you came in and he was gone."

Bogarde looked around, maybe searching for the banker.

"We have a worse problem," Desiree repeated.

"What problem?"

She looked around now. "Not out here in the street. Let's get something to eat."

The Clover Grill was closest and wasn't crowded. They took the table at the back of the place and gave their orders to a listless waitress.

"What problem?" Bogarde had lowered his voice.

"Signore Badalamente came into my dressing room and warned me, warned you actually, to stop doing what we're doing."

"Doing?"

The waitress brought Bogarde's beer and Desiree's ginger ale.

Desiree leaned closer. "They know."

"About what?"

"About Elmer and if we pull the jewelry thing, they'll know that too."

Bogarde actually smiled as he leaned back, took a hit of beer and then said, "They don't know shit."

Could he be this stupid?

"And so what if they do?"

She leaned close again. "They're Mafia."

"Ha. Like the New York Mafia? That's a crock. This is the Deep South, lady, they don't have that kinda muscle down here."

Bogarde hadn't seen Baddie's eyes.

"I can take care of myself," Bogarde assured her. "And they won't touch you. You're their blond desire."

The burgers came quick and Desiree thought she couldn't eat until she took the first bite. It was so delicious, she ate. Bogarde devoured his burger.

"I learned how to handle people that like in Joliet. I ain't backing down. Gangsters don't back down." He smiled now.

After, Bogarde dropped her off and didn't try to come up. As he pulled away, he told her they had to remain focused on the caper and she wondered what the other woman looked like. Was she one of the older dames Bogarde preyed on, or had he found a replacement for her.

She thought about it on the way upstairs but forgot about Bogarde completely as she took a long, warm bubble bath.

• • •

Jim didn't expect Desiree to be sitting on the front stoop outside his apartment when he got off that morning. She stood as he arrived and just looked into his eyes. She wore another sundress, this one pink, and followed him inside, where she pulled herself to him and kissed him, long and hard. They hadn't touched each other for a couple days and the passion came up fast.

After, lying in his bed, a light early-morning breeze filtering through the window screens, Desiree said, "Badalamente and Fat Sal. They're the real Mafia, right? Like Lucky Luciano."

"That's what Leo tells me." He looked at her. "Has Badalamente been bothering you?"

"No. Not at all. I just wondered."

After a minute, Jim added, "Leo says they don't get along. The Badalamentes and the Cardonas, Fat Sal and his father Silver Dollar Sam."

"Are these guys like the New York Mafia? You know, dumping bodies in the East River."

Jim shrugged. "Dump a body in the Mississippi, you'll never find it. By the time it comes up it'll be in the gulf."

Jim was just glad he'd gone straight home, instead of picking up the papers and heading for breakfast. He lay in his bed, thinking about what he wanted to tell Desiree but when he looked at her again, her eyes were closed and her breathing nice and easy. He closed his eyes and tried to sleep only something fluttered in his belly. It was the same flutter he felt just before a battle, just before they'd started across the Hürtgen, just before the panzers came through the Ardennes, north of Bastogne in the dead of winter.

• • •

Desiree was late and hurried around the corner, her purse slapping against her side as she passed a sitting cab. She spotted Leo walking her way. He shook his head as he came to her and she saw police cars parked in front of Hotsy Jazz, red lights flashing. Leo took her hand and led her back around the corner.

They stopped and he said, "Fat Sal got whacked a couple hours ago. In his office." He shook his head again. "Nobody heard anything. Day-shift bar-back found him. Shot in the head, still in his chair behind his desk."

Desiree felt her throat tighten. Leo held up an envelope for her.

"Paycheck," he said. "Badalamente is in there," Leo shaking his head again, "he's writing paychecks as the cops are asking questions."

"He's in there?"

"Man has an iron clad alibi. Cops brought him straight from jail. He was booked last night for driving while intoxicated and spent the night in the drunk tank." Leo took her hand again and started to lead her away.

"Won't the cops think it's suspicious if I don't show up?"

Leo stopped. "Yeah. I guess."

As Desiree pulled her hand away, Leo said, "I'll wait for you. Then we'll go over to tell Jim."

She started to leave, stopped and reached into her purse. She stepped closer to Leo and passed him the Detective Special. His eyes opened wide as he slipped it into his pants pocket. Desiree stopped a few steps away, took in a breath before continuing.

A cop in a uniform stopped her at the door with, "Who are you?"

"I work here."

"Let her in," growled a voice from inside and Desiree stepped in to see several men in ill-fitting suits standing inside. Toward one side, away from the bar, sat Alphonso Badalamente with a black-haired man with a cigarette dangling from his lips. The man looked like Zorro, without the mask.

A squat man with stubby arms, in a rumpled brown suit, waddled over and said, "What's your name, whore?"

The man had dull gray eyes with lids only half-opened and wore his stringy brown hair like Moe, from The Three Stooges.

"Hey!" The man barked, "You deaf?"

"No. I'm not a whore."

"Yeah?" the man took a step toward her and another detective, this one about six feet, with short carrot-red hair and too many freckles came around the squat man as the Zorro-looking detective called out, "Hays! Go outside and watch the cars. Make sure nobody steals them."

The squat man wheeled, huffed and mumbled a curse but left, shoving over a chair on the way out. The redheaded detective, opened his coat to show Desiree his gold star-and-crescent badge. "I'm Det. Willie Spade. Who are you?"

"Desiree Blanc." She looked over at the day bartender, the young one whose name she could never remember and asked for a club soda. "You want something to drink?" she asked Spade as she slipped over to the bar, putting her purse atop.

Spade followed and nodded to the bartender. "Coke." He picked up her purse and glanced in it.

"Just making sure you're not packing heat," said Spade with a smile.

"Actually, my real name is Dorothy Jellnick."

Spade took out a notepad.

"I'm twenty-five. From Wolf's Bark, Mississippi. That's up in Wayne County, north Miss-ssippi. I've worked here at Hotsy Jazz for a little over a year. I strip."

Spade kept writing notes.

"Now, can you tell me what happened? I mean, is this a raid?" Desiree was surprised at how calm she felt.

Spade had deep-set brown eyes, a shade lighter than Jim's. He had a whimsical look on his face as she said, "Your boss. Salvatore 'Fat Sal' Cardona was murdered in his office about four hours ago."

Desiree was proud of the way she gave him a shocked look, as if she'd just heard, as if she was suddenly frightened to be in a place where a man was killed. She should be in Hollywood.

"Where were you around noon?"

"Having lunch with my landlady, Mrs. Watson." Desiree picked up her purse. "I have her phone number. She invited me for cucumber sandwiches. Ever have cucumber sandwiches? It's actually the cream cheese that makes it."

Desiree had showered at Jim's after a good nap and as she got home, Mrs. Watson stepped out and invited her for a light lunch.

"I was with Jim Munster before that, at his apartment on Marigny Street from about eight-thirty until shortly before noon when I went home. His landlady can verify it. She was peeking out at us when we went in and when I left. Busybody. Jim works here as a bar-back." She read Mrs. Watson's phone number to Spade, along with Jim's address for his landlady.

"You were at this Munster's place?"

"Yes. We did it and feel asleep after."

Spade smiled as he wrote it down, his lips mouthing, 'we did it'.

"When's the last time you saw Fat Sal?"

"Tuesday night, I think. He walked out of his office and out the place."

"When's the last time you saw Alphonso Badalamente?"

"A minute ago, when I came in."

Spade looked up from his notes, chuckled lightly. "Before that."

She looked past his shoulder at Baddie who was still talking to the Zorro-looking detective.

"Last night, just before midnight. In my dressing room. We talked about scheduling."

"What time was that?"

"Just before midnight."

Spade nodded. "What about his brother, Carlo?"

"Haven't seen him in over a week."

"What about Sammy Tulipano?"

"Who?"

"He's called Sammy the Turtle?"

"Oh. Haven't seen him this week at all. They come and go. Don't answer to me."

Spade chuckled louder this time and took a sip of Coke. He passed her a business card and told her she could go. The place would probably be closed a couple days. As he stepped away, he turned back and said, "You know what Tulipano means in Italian?"

She shrugged.

Spade called out, "Hey lieutenant. What's Tulipano mean again?

"Tulip," answered the Zorro twin.

"Tulip," Spade repeated. He seemed to get a kick out of that.

• • •

"Perfect," Bogarde said. "We'll make our move Friday. Just as planned. They're all tied up with this murder, now, your Mafia guys."

"I don't know. Badalamente meant what he said."

"Sure. But how they gonna know it's us and like I said, they got cops all over them. It's all over the evening paper." Bogarde sounded awfully sure of himself. "I told you before. Timing's everything in a heist."

She'd seen the paper at Jim's, Fat Sal's picture on page one, along with pictures of his father, Silver Dollar Sam Cardona and Alphonso 'Baddie' Badalamente. One reporter speculated that since Silver Dollar Sam was not whacked, that he would do one of the rarest things a Mafioso could do. Retire alive.

Baddie was clearly the new boss, although he did have legal problems now, including a hard look from U.S. Immigration who wanted to deport him to Sicily. Baddie's lawyer had already countered that move, saying the birth certificate used by Immigration was a forgery and that Alphonso Badalamente, unlike his brother Carlo who was born in Sicily, was born in Alabama. For some odd reason, Costa Rica was prepared to take Badalamente.

"This is more convoluted than Roswell," said Leo as they had gathered around the paper in Jim's apartment. That was when the two men went off about flying saucers and sounded like little boys. Desiree re-read the news articles.

Alphonso Badalamente had only been arrested once, before the drunk driving charge, and that was when he was eighteen. Extortion. Charges dropped by the victim. Fat Sal had an extensive record, from pandering to shoplifting to armed robbery. No convictions. Silver Dollar Sam had been arrested for murder twice. No convictions.

Carlo Badalamente had been arrested for armed robbery, simple robbery and well as kidnapping, as was Sammy 'The Turtle' Tulipano. The only conviction was Carlo's simple robbery charge back in 1938.

A big picture of Hotsy Jazz on the front of the paper would bring in customers like never before. No doubt. The place was now infamous. The picture was a night shot of the front of the place, a gas street lamp on the left of the frame with a Bourbon St. street sign, the awning atop the front doorway reading 'Hotsy Jazz' – 'Striptease' – 'Continuous Entertainment'. A black silhouette of a naked woman on the wall next to the door read '16 Beautiful Ladies. New Orleans Nite Life at its Best in ONE SPOT'.

"So," Leo said when she'd finished with the paper. "What's with the gun?" He nodded to the Detective Special sitting on Jim's small kitchen table.

Desiree winked and gave her best impersonation of Jean Harlow. "You two aren't always around to protect little ole' me."

• • •

Desiree needed the raincoat in the drizzle on Friday. It was eleven a.m., as Bogarde had called and moved up the heist. He had to take an early lunch that day.

Standing under a balcony at the corner of St. Ann and Dauphine, her hair teased out again, she had trouble spotting Bogarde's car while she wore the dark sunglasses. Behind her the man at the newsstand hawked her out big time. She'd bought a *Hollywood Photoplay* magazine when she'd walked up, so the man would think she was really there to buy a magazine. When Bogarde pulled up and had to tap the horn because she didn't recognize the car, she figured the busybodies at the corner would just conclude this was a clandestine rendezvous and not preparation for a heist.

"Told you," Bogarde said as they reached the corner of Chartres and Madison as there were two open parking spots right there. He pulled in, killed the engine and tugged on the gorilla mask. They'd passed Roth Jewelers and saw the old men inside, but no customers.

Desiree got out the passenger side and tip-toed back to the banquette and didn't see Bogarde but heard a curse. He'd slipped on his ass and jumped up quickly and had to readjust the mask which had twisted, covering his eyes.

"You're gonna need that." Desiree pointed to his forty-five which lay in the rain.

"Goddammit!" Bogarde scooped up his gun and wiped it on his pants leg as they headed across Chartres for Roth Jewelers.

"The raincoat!" Bogarde snapped.

Desiree said, "I know." She waited until they were in front of the jewelers to drop the raincoat and stroll into the place in the see-through teddy, black stocking and garter belt. She immediately bumped into a glass case. The place was so damn dark, she could barely see through the sunglasses.

She had to tap down the glasses to see over the top – what was that? Gleeking! – as Bogarde brushed past her, screaming, "This is the 'beauty-and-the-beast gang'! Stick 'em up!"

Stick 'em up? Son-of-a-bitch thought was Cagney.

"Gemme all the money." Bogarde reached the desks where the two old men sat and waved his forty-five from one to the other. They men blinked back at them from behind identical black framed glasses with lenses as thick as the bottom of a Coke bottle.

"OK! OK! Schvartza! I'll get the money. I'll get the money." The midget on the left got up slowly and headed for a black safe, which was half open.

"Watch him!" Bogarde barked as he went to the first glass case, looked at it, having to adjust his mask again, then smashed it with his gun.

"No!" screeched the second midget. "Don't break de case. They come all de way from Prague!" The second midget waved his arms around. "De jewels and de money. Dey insured. But not de cases."

Desiree turned her attention to the man at the safe. When he turned back, his eyes were level with her tits and he leered right at them. She pulled out the Detective Special and said, "The money!"

He brought out a green strong box staring at the Colt now as he stepped back to his desk where he dropped the box, flipped open the lid.

"Back away," she told him and he obeyed. He was staring at her chest again. She scooped the bills out of the box, went around the desk and pulled a drawer and found a big envelope which she filled.

"Now. The loose jewels. The diamonds," she said to the first midget, pointing the gun at him again.

"A gun! Where'd you get a gun?" Bogarde called out.

"Shut up!" She stepped forward, cocking the hammer on the Detective Special and pressed it again the man's nose.

"OK. OK." The man backed to a small closet that was hard to spot and took out a key ring.

"Hurry up, old man," she said, squeezing the beveled wooden grip of the Colt, which felt hot in her hand.

He unlocked the closet and backed away. She went to it and saw velvet-lined drawers and pulled each out. There were diamonds, emeralds, rubies and every type of semi-precious stone she could imagine, most wrapped in cellophane.

She hurried back to get an even bigger envelope and hurried filling it, dumping the jewels inside. The old man was looking down at her crotch now. She made sure she got every loose jewel.

"I can see your bush," the man said and actually smiled.

She gleeked the man again and the man moved his head to the side, like dog did when it wanted to get a better look at something. As she walked away, she rolled her ass at him, then snatched up a couple big bags to take to Bogarde who had picked jewelry from the first glass case and was rifling the second case as the second midget had unlocked it for him.

He stuffed both envelopes she'd brought and she said, "This is enough."

"I know." Bogarde had both arms filled with the bags, his forty-five in his upturned right hand. Desiree had her bags cradled but managed to level the Colt at the midgets who were both standing now in the center of the aisle, both staring at her body.

"I'll get the car," Bogarde said, hurrying out. "Cover them." He dropped one bag and his gun had to pick them up as he went for the car. Desiree covered the Roth brothers who seemed content to just stand and look at her.

Bogarde backed the Ford out of the parking spot and she slipped the Detective Special into her purse and hurried out, scooping the raincoat up on the way to the car. Bogarde gunned it and the car raced down Madison Street, stopping at the end of the block for a moment at the stop sign before Bogarde turned right and got into the traffic on Decatur Street.

"You can take off the mask now," she said as she climbed into the raincoat.

He yanked off the mask and his hair was sticking straight up. He checked himself out in the rear view mirror and almost rear-ended a Chevrolet. He had such a maniacal look on his face. Desiree saw she was breathing heavily as Bogarde turned up Bienville Street. Stopping at each stop sign, he looked back and forth, then gunned the car.

"You might want to slow down," she said.

"I know. I know." He tried but she could see he was too fired up. Thankfully they saw no cop cars as they turned right and headed through the Quarter, driving straight to her place. He found a parking spot right in front and Desiree heard Mrs. Watson call out, "My-o-my. Grocery shopping in the middle of the day."

Desiree guessed the bags looked like grocery bags. But she stopped immediately as that same gray DeSoto went past with the dark haired man in it, the one looked like a detective and he looked at her as he passed.

Soon as they closed the door to her room, Desiree tossed off the rain coat and they moved to the coffee table to dig everything from the bags. She put the loose gems in separate piles while Bogarde piled up the jewelry, bracelets, necklaces and rings, all women's jewelry.

She counted the cash twice. Three thousand, two hundred and forty four dollars. That was sixteen hundred, twenty two bucks each. She counted fifty-two loose diamonds, twenty six emeralds, forty rubies and sixty six sapphires. There were less semi-precious stones, which she divided evenly. No way either could tell which were the better diamonds, so they went by size, same with the emeralds, rubies and sapphires.

"We'll have to dig the stones out of the bracelets and rings," said Bogarde when they'd finished divvying up the loot. He'd brushed his hair down with his hands and sat there with a flushed face.

Desiree could feel her heart stammering as they sat on the floor on either side of the coffee table. Bogarde started taking off his tie and it struck her.

"Hey, weren't you supposed to go back to work?"

"Dammit." He got up and went downstairs to call in sick, she supposed.

When he stepped back in, Desiree was on her sofa, on her back and naked. He locked the door and took off his clothes in a big hurry. She pointed to the rubber she'd laid out on the end table while he was on the phone.

The sex was explosive. It was actually the first time she'd had sex with Bogarde since she'd started with Jim and it was the best sex she'd had with Bogarde for quite a while. Both were juiced from the stick-up, she supposed as they lay entwined on the sofa after, trying to catch their breaths.

The heat got them up later and they showered together before going back out to the living room where Bogarde put his half of the loot in two of the bags before getting dressed. Desiree sat naked on the sofa and ran a towel through her hair.

"We having dinner?" she said, wondering what he'd say.

"I … uh. Have you seen my gun?" He had his pants, sock and shoes on.

She peeked out from the towel and watched him look around the living room, watched him throw on his shirt and hurry out as she said, "Did you leave it in the car?"

He came back up ten minutes later, looking pale. He snatched up his bags of loot and his tie and stood there staring at her.

She leaned back on the sofa and said, "Tell me you didn't leave your gun behind."

Chapter 10
THAT'S BECAUSE EVERYONE THINKS I'M A REDHEAD

Desiree caught a cab and made it to the Whitney Bank in time to put the loot into her safety deposit box. The redheaded bank officer spotted her coming in and eagerly helped her.

"What was the name of that movie you were in?"

It took a second for her to remember. "Oh, *The Harvey Girls*."

"Yeah. Wish it was still out," he smiled and continued flirting with her, telling her she smelled nice this time. He was trying. She also dropped by the post office and got a money order for two hundred to send to Wolf's Bark.

Rain threatened again as Desiree made it home, knocking gently on Mrs. Watson's door. Her landlady opened it immediately.

"I'm sorry," Desiree apologized, seeing the landlady in a thick robe, her hair wrapped in a towel. "I can come back."

"Don't be silly. Would you like a cup of tea?"

"That would be nice." Desiree stepped into the pristine room and noticed the flowery smell, only no flowers. As she followed Mrs. Watson into the kitchen, she realized the smells came from scented candles. A purple candle was lit but there were a dozen others unlit around the living room.

Mrs. Watson's kitchen faced Frenchmen Street and was brightly lit from too many windows. The white curtains were closed but they were thin enough to let in the brilliant late afternoon sunlight. Mrs. Watson's Formica table was pink Formica with chrome legs. Desiree sat in one of the four matching chairs as the landlady poured two cups of tea.

"Just made this. It's chamomile actually." She brought the fancy cup and saucers and put them on the table next to a matching sugar bowl. "Soothes the stomach and bowels," Mrs. Watson said as she sat. "It's also a sleep aid. No caffeine, like regular tea."

The chamomile was delicious without sugar, although Mrs. Watson took two teaspoons.

"I wonder if you could do me a favor," said Desiree.

"Of course, child. What is it?"

Desiree dug a small envelope out of her purse. She opened it and showed Mrs. Watson the key.

"It's to my safety deposit box.

"Safety deposit box? Oh, my."

"I work around some bad elements and I know it'll be safe with you."

Mrs. Watson gave her a long stare, her brow furrowing slightly. "You think someone might sneak into your room?"

"Anything's possible." What Desiree couldn't say was she was more afraid of the cops barging in and ransacking her room. She'd been worried ever since those cops had checked her out after they'd jacked up Elmer and seeing those cops and firemen just before they pulled their jewelry heist prodded her to do something. Not to mention the man in the DeSoto. She didn't want to leave it in her boarding room and wasn't about to carry it around with her. Now that she had some real loot in the box, she wanted that key safe. A gun-moll didn't leave stuff lying around.

Desiree put the key back into the envelope and slid it toward Mrs. Watson, who picked it right up and said, "Follow me, dear." They went back into the living room, straight to a wall of built-in bookshelves where Mrs. Watson reached up and dropped the envelope behind some books.

"In case anything happens to me, it'll be behind *The Great Gatsby* and *Tender is the Night.*" She turned and patted Desiree's hand. "And when you need the key to get in and out of the box, just come on by. You know, unless I'm at the grocery, I'm here." Mrs. Watson looked back at the books. "I just adore F. Scott Fitzgerald." She led the way back into the kitchen. "Poor man died thinking himself a failure. We're in the middle of a revival of his works. You really should read him."

Desiree smiled as she sat to finish her tea. It was nice there in the kitchen with Mrs. Watson. Her kitchen back in Wolf's Bark was never this cozy, never this clean. There was always red dirt on the floor back home. Her mother never had the time to make anything this pristine, nor time for a leisurely spot of tea in the early evening, much less reading about some guy called Gatsby.

Maybe the chamomile would settle the butterflies bouncing in her stomach. She'd felt jittery since Bogarde left. Not that she wanted him around, but being alone, she just felt jittery. She'd resisted calling Jim but as she finished the tea, she knew she would and did from the hallway.

"I'll be right over."

"No," she said. "I'll be right over."

"Fine."

As she walked beneath the threatening clouds, she thought – *two men at the same time?*

Jesus Christ.

• • •

Jim and Desiree got off the St. Charles streetcar at Audubon Park, Desiree looking over her shoulder at the spires of Loyola University and the gothic-looking church attached to it.

"Place looks like a castle," she said.

"Except for the red brick," Jim said. The front of the university had a horseshoe driveway which faced the avenue. A large white statue of Jesus with his arms open seemed to peer over at the park. The buildings running alongside the drive had archways and a parapet running atop and did look like a castle. Tulane University next door was made of tan field stone, looking like pictures Jim had seen of Ivy League schools back east.

It was a bright Saturday, late morning, and cardinals danced along the bushes next to the lagoon in Audubon Park as Jim and Desiree strolled away from the avenue across plush green grass and beneath a sky that was a deep blue, a darker shade of blue than normal, the clouds fluffed out, looking like cotton candy.

They didn't speak, didn't need to, thought Jim. It felt so natural being together, walking side by side, soaking in the sunshine, feeling relaxed even with his heart pattering as it always did around Desiree. She walked slowly, in deference to his limp, he was sure. And she seemed at ease, calm and peaceful today. Desiree Blanc looked radiant in the sunlight, her hair styled straight and parted so her right eye was partially hidden, Veronica Lake peek-a-boo style. Of course Desiree was much taller but she had that gorgeous face and twinkle in her eye like Veronica in *I Married a Witch*.

He wondered what she was thinking.

Desiree was thinking about the twenty-two diamonds in her safety deposit box, and the fourteen emeralds of various sizes and various cuts, and the twenty rubies, some the deepest red she'd ever seen, and the sapphires, garnets, opals and the blue stones with the gold specks Bogarde called lapis. She had over five thousand dollars in cash in the box, more money than she'd ever imagine she'd have at one time.

She was thinking of how upset Bogarde was that morning, coming over early, coming over with the morning paper, not even noticing she was getting ready to leave, maybe meet another man.

"Did you see the goddamn paper?"

"No. And quit shouting." She lowered her voice, hoping he'd follow along. "My landlady's a lady and …"

Bogarde waved the newspaper over his head like a mad-man. "They're calling us the 'beast-and-the-beauty'. They got it backwards, goddamn Roth brothers!"

Desiree giggled. "Why are you complaining, you get top billing?"

"And you're a freakin' redhead. A naked freakin' *natural* redhead. Son-of-a-bitches are blind as bats." Bogarde began pacing, explaining how the Roth brothers weren't sure but the Beast *might* have been wearing a mask. "Might have! What the hell else?" He wheeled, twisting the paper in the air. "They said either I wore a mask or I was ugly as shit!"

"They didn't say *shit* in the paper." Desiree began the slow process of contour-painting her lips.

"They said …" he untwisted the paper. "It's right here." It took him nearly a minute to find it. "The man was either in a mask or was ugly as hell."

He twisted the paper around again. "It said we took a small fortune in cash and jewelry. There's a ten thousand dollar reward for the capture of the 'beast-and-the-beauty duo'. We're not a *duo*. We're a gang!"

Desiree looked him in the eye and he froze in place, glaring back at her as she asked, "Did they say anything about your gun?"

Bogarde looked like a balloon deflating. His shoulders fell and his jaw went slack. His entire face sagged. He let the newspaper tumble to the floor. Eventually he said, "Yeah. The 'beast-and-the-beauty' left one of their guns behind, a full-loaded forty-five that police were comparing to guns used in other robberies."

It wasn't until Desiree picked up her purse did he even realize she was leaving.

"Where you going?"

"Shopping on Canal Street. Wanna come along?"

He shook his head and she led the way out. He followed her downstairs and sagged again when she asked, "You dumped the jewelry by now, haven't you?"

"Of course."

She didn't turn to see if he was lying. She didn't believe him. The man was dumb enough to keep the distinctive pieces that the police could identify in a heartbeat.

"You better keep them hidden for a long, long time," she said.

"I dumped them."

Stepping into the sunshine, she turned back and said, "A natural redhead, huh?"

He nodded forlornly.

"Maybe I should dye my hair ash blond," she said factiously, pirouetted and walked away.

Strolling now as she and Jim crossed Magazine Street, she realized they were in the zoo already. The Audubon Zoo was actually pretty big and spread out from Magazine all the way to the railroad tracks next to the river. They headed for a large pavilion with marble columns surrounding a huge pool with a black fence around it.

Feeding time for the seals drew a crowd, mostly kids who pressed their face against the fence to watch a man and a woman in khakis feed the seals, who were actually sea lions according to the brass plaque attached to the fence.

"They are fast," Jim said as the sea lions streaked under water and dove *out* of the water to the tarmac for a fishy snack. It wasn't exact a staged act, may not have been choreographed as the two handlers were kept busy turning back and forth feeding sea lions who never stopped moving.

"I expected alligators," Desiree said taking Jim's hand as they strolled away.

"I think there's a reptile section."

There was, in a brick building, but the alligators were outside, in a shallow rock pool, about three dozen of them lying fat and half submerged in murky water. Several had feet missing and all looked too sluggish to pose any danger.

Desiree felt sorry for the monkeys in their small cages and felt even sorrier for the herd of little light brown monkeys on Monkey Island. They just sat there and watched the humans pass. For some reason, she couldn't find the gorillas and asked a zookeeper.

"They went to another zoo," he said.

"Which zoo?"

"I dunno. Want me to go ask?"

Desiree shook her head. She'd seen enough gorilla looks from the men at Hotsy Jazz anyway.

The dens of the big cats were a little bigger, especially the tigers and lions but the leopard and black panther were completely enclosed in cages.

"They could climb out of anything," Jim said. "You want a panther loose in the city?"

Peacocks ran loose around the place, along with pheasants with their wings clipped. The otter pool was entertaining at least but Desiree didn't like the zoo all that much and jumped when a stray raccoon pop out from under a bush and loped away. The coon was probably not part of any exhibit, but a native species who wandered through the wide zoo. A thunder clap turned Jim and Desiree away from the river and they moved back through the park, keeping close to the gazebos in case the rain caught them again. It didn't.

They took the streetcar to the Camellia Grill and Harry greeted them with a wide smile and said, "Your wishes are my desire. Good to see you again, ma'am."

Jim glanced at Desiree who said, "I'm sort of a regular."

"I only wished," said Harry as he passed them menus, then brought icy waters and held their straws until they pulled the straw out from the wrapper, which he tossed with another big grin. Maybe he was hoping for another peek up her dress. She laughed to herself.

"Great burgers," Desiree said, "and the best milk shakes this side of the Vatican."

"They have milk shakes at the Vatican?"

"Sure they do," Harry injected. "How you think dem cardinals got so fat?"

They were half finished their burgers when two patrolmen came in. Little '3' on their collars. These were French Quarter cops from the Third Precinct. Both gave Desiree a glance and glanced at her a couple more times but that was all they did. Then again, they were looking for a redhead, weren't they?

• • •

The next week was the strangest Desiree spent at Hotsy Jazz. Leo seemed to be in charge but actually no one was in charge. The place just went on. Like clockwork, everyone a cog in the well-oiled operation that had no problems, didn't even need the bouncers. The crowds were small the night the place re-opened but the next night it was popping with a newer, better looking class of curious, including more women than ever before.

"Murder draws crowds," Leo told Desiree and Jim Wednesday night. "I hear there are Jack the Ripper tours in London. Tourist go see where the women were butchered."

By Desiree's last night of work that week, Friday, the place was popping and two new bouncers had materialized. They had New York accents, or maybe Jersey accents, were big and overweight with a scarier than usual look to them, one with a scarred, pock-marked face. They were unsmiling and looked lifeless, like something from a late night monster movie.

Desiree and Jim saw three matinees that week.

The Bachelor and the Bobby Soxer with Cary Grant, Myrna Loy and Shirley Temple, who'd become a teenager and played one with a crush on a confirmed bachelor, harassing him and what does he do? Falls for her sister, a judge.

The Secret Life of Walter Mitty with Danny Kaye and sultry, hot, vamp blond, Virginia Mayo.

"I swear she's cross-eyed," said Desiree as they left the Saenger Theatre. "Not a lot, just slightly."

Jim almost fell over and she reached for him, thinking it was his foot but he was convulsed with laughter. It took a while for him to ask, "Slightly? Slightly? How can she be slightly cross-eyed?"

"You can only see it at certain angles," Desiree said stiffly, walking away so Jim would have to catch up. "She's semi-cross-eyed," Desiree called out over her shoulder. "You weren't looking at her eyes."

"Nope. I wasn't."

The last was a drama, *Dead Reckoning* with Humphrey Bogart and Lizabeth Scott.

"He's just better with Bacall," Jim said.

"I don't like Lizabeth Scott," Desiree said, tucking her arm around Jim's as they left the Orpheum. "She has a deep voice like Bacall, but her eyes are too squinty."

"At least they aren't crossed."

She elbowed him in the side but hung on in case his foot gave out, which it didn't.

On Thursday night, Bogarde picked Desiree up after work, but didn't touch her. He seemed better, gaining some of his confidence back, maybe a little swagger.

"Told you," he said when he dropped her off after their late-night meal. "You bosses don't know everything that happens in the city. Told you they didn't have the kinda moxie to catch us."

"That's because everyone thinks I'm a redhead."

On Friday there was a note waiting on Desiree's dressing table.

"Don't forget Schroeder tomorrow. T will meet you outside." The note was signed 'B'.

• • •

Turtle wore a white turtle neck on a day that was too-hot for a turtle neck. He wore it out, over his pants and Desiree was sure there was a gun under it somewhere, probably along the small of his back. He spotted her crossing Royal Street, nodded and led the way to Schroeder's door.

They went in without knocking and found Schroeder with two cameras on tripods and a tall man with skin the color of licorice.

"Desiree Blanc, meet Reverend Ardin Clavell. He's a big fan."

The Negro looked to be in his mid-forties with prematurely graying hair and a white bead that stood out on stark contrast to his skin. His handshake was gently and his eyes kind.

"A fan?" she said. "When have you seen me, reverend?"

"Call me Ardin. I've seen your photos and heard about your act and I'm very grateful you agreed to pose with me."

Turtle perched himself on a stool just inside the doorway when Schroeder moved his tripods across the wide room to a red sofa. Just beyond the sofa was a table with a silver wine bucket, a bottle protruding and two wine glasses.

"I thought a little Liebfrauenmilch would be nice," said the reverend as he reached for the wine bottle. "It comes from vineyards near the city of Worms in West Germany." He filled both glasses and handed one to Desiree. "It's from the vineyards of the Church of Our Lady of the Rhineland-Palantinate."

Desiree took a sip and the wine was sweet and light.

"It's a high quality hock of very limited distribution," the reverend went on. "Worms is an important city. It's where Martin Luther defended his case against Emperor Charles V.

Desiree took another sip before saying, "Don't tell me, you're Lutheran?"

"Minister of the Jesus Christ Lutheran Church of the New Nazarene. What denomination are you, Miss Blanc?"

"Grew up Baptist but now I'm just Hotsy Jazz."

That brought a wide grin.

She almost asked what happened to the old Nazarene but didn't know if the man had a sense of humor about religion. He had roaming eyes all right, looking her up and down, which almost made her giggle because he was about to see a lot more.

"What I'd like to start with is having you both disrobe, standing next to each other. Go slowly so I can focus and shoot."

The reverend, she preferred to think of him as 'the reverend' rather than his name because she felt her heart rising, knowing she was stripping with a man of the cloth. He wore a blue shirt over dress pants, but started with his loafers and socks as she stepped out of her mules.

Desiree, in a pale green blouse and red sarong skirt, simply unwrapped the skirt and stood there in her white panties for Schroeder to photograph them.

"Good," he said. "I'll say freeze and y'all just stop."

She took off her blouse as the reverend took off his shirt. He wore no undershirt and his muscles were toned nicely. They froze for a photos then she freed her breasts and he let out a low gasp as he leered at them. He dropped his pants. He wore jockeys and was already excited.

Another photo and off went panties and jockeys. Schroeder had them stand side by side facing him, then turn around for rear shots. He had them stand back to back, their asses almost touching, then face to face.

They posed on the sofa, her reclining and him kneeling next to her. The reverend wasn't looking into her eyes much now, but checked out her body parts. At one point, she thought he was trying to count her pubic hair.

Desiree knew men were visually attracted to women, figured cave-women strutted in front of cave men to get their attention, maybe give them a peek up their loin cloths. She knew a good looking guy usually got a gal's attention. But she'd been learning, watching Jim and sometimes Bogarde and now with this man, that the naked male body did something to her. It got her juices flowing and she liked looking.

They went out back to the patio and posed around the tree and flowers, then went back inside for more photos. Schroeder got a little more provocative, having her spread her legs as she lay draped over the sofa.

"Can you tweak your nipples?" he asked.

She tweaked them.

When he asked her to do it again a little later, she said, "It'll work better if *you* tweaked them."

Schroeder almost blushed and she saw the reverend ready and willing but there was no touching between the models, so Schroeder had the task of feeling up her breasts to get the nipples hard.

She didn't look at Turtle until they were getting dressed. For a moment she thought he was scowling at her, certainly disapproving of this white girl naked with a Negro, but he wasn't scowling at all. He wasn't even looking at her in particular, but rather at the windows behind, but when he realized she was looking at him, turned to her, his eyes rising.

"Y'all done?" He got off the stool.

Schroeder told him, yes.

Turtle just nodded and moved to the door and waited.

Schroeder thanked Desiree three more times and the reverend bowed to her and told her it was a most splendid way to spend an afternoon.

Down on the street Turtle turned to her and said, "See ya' around kid. You really are a gorgeous filly." And he walked off, pulling up his belt and she was sure she saw a bulge on his hip.

Bogarde lived closer but it was Saturday and he was at work so she went straight to Jim's. When he opened the door, in only a pair of shorts, she stepped in, kissed his mouth and yanked down his shorts.

• • •

Bogarde had the loot laid out on his kitchen table, diamonds, emeralds, rubies, sapphires, lapis. The six necklaces, fifteen rings and nine bracelets sat in a separate pile. He'd just recounted the stones and made sure he and Desiree had split them evenly and picked up the needle-nosed pliers to extricate the diamonds, rubies and garnets from the necklaces and rings.

"Make sure you get rid of the jewelry," Desiree had nagged him. He was pretty sure she'd counted the rings and necklaces but didn't count the number of stones in each necklaces and since he was doing the work, he'd get a few more that she would get.

Dropping the broken jewelry in a garbage can would be no problem, but fencing the gem stones would be. In the movies it was easy to find a fence. In real life, no way, and the only people Bogarde knew who knew fences were the Badalamentes and that was the last place he'd go with this. Even without the threat, not that he was afraid of them, the Guineas would just steal everything from him.

So Bogarde's plan was to sock away the gems for a rainy day, maybe find a crooked jeweler shopping for a used car one day – at Bogarde's Used Cars. He and Fannie decided on the name the previous evening, lying on her bed side by side after a little tryst.

"Your name belongs in neon lights," she'd said.

They had gone back to the parking lot she owned at the corner of Tulane Avenue and South Villere. The little building where the attendant sat to keep warm in winter had to go. Fannie already had an architect, one of her many cousins, drawing up a new building.

He put Desiree's share of the stones from the necklaces and bracelets in an envelope, put his stones in separate envelopes and tucked them into an empty Luzianne coffee can, sealing the top with tape. He went to the pantry and sat on the floor and carefully pried away what once was a loose board at the back of the pantry. There wasn't much room, but enough for the can, which he slid inside and nailed the board into place.

He'd give Desiree her cut when he saw her again, which wouldn't be today. He was glad their passion was waning because after the bank job, he planned to ease away from her. Not cut her off completely, of course. He may need her again.

It irked him, that crack about him getting top billing with the 'beast-and-the-beauty'. For the bank heist, he planned to leave a note that explained the correct name of his gang.

• • •

The morning paper on that bright, warm Sunday, July twenty-seventh, ran another Roswell story. Jim read it over coffee while Desiree slept in the bedroom. It was mostly a re-hash of the latest from the *Santa Fe Pueblo*, but the associated press reporter added a couple interesting side notes. First the debris – unlike anything the 'highly trained' army personnel had seen before, was flown to three different government installations. Second – a 'government official' confiscated the notes from two reporters and warned a radio reporter not to play the interview he'd recorded from a ranch hand from the Foster Ranch. Men involved with the recovery have been ordered to never talk to about the incident.

Desiree came out sleepy-eyed, completely naked and sat on Jim's lap, wrapping her arms around his neck, cuddling against him. She felt sleepy-warm and her hair was a mess, sheet lines marked that gorgeous body.

"I'm a wreck," she said.

"Yeah. Right."

They took a long shower together in a tub that wasn't big enough and got the floor wet and took their time getting ready to go out to another matinee at the Famous Theatre, *The Purple Monster Strikes*. The show wasn't very crowded. The purple monster was a Martian whose spacecraft crashed near the place where Earth's first spaceship was being built. The survivor was actually the first of an invading army, posing as a human to get control of the earth's spaceship project. There was secret service man and a cute brunette and the movie was actually a compilation of a serial that ran right after the war.

"Well, we had to hit a clunker sooner or later," said Desiree as she wrapped her arm around his. They strolled down the Esplanade neutral ground, moving from side to side to skirt the trees. Jim thought the movie was pretty good, for science fiction.

"Recognize the brunette?" he asked.

"Nope."

"She was the Tiger Woman in the Republic Serials during the war. Wore a short leopard-skin skirt outfit. Pretty sexy."

"The Tiger Woman wore leopard skin?"

"Yep."

"I've never seen those actors before."

"I have but I can't remember where."

A voice called out and they looked to their right. It was Thomas, uh Tennessee, waving at them and holding hands with a truly attractive brunette woman in a tight, blood-red dress.

"I have someone you *must* meet!"

They crossed the avenue and as they arrived at the couple, Thomas said, "Young lovers, allow me to introduce you to my newest friend who happens to be a love sorceress."

Jim didn't mean to stare but those light green eyes looked directly into his in a way most women wouldn't stare into a man's eyes. They were filled with innocence, so much it was disarming and he could say nothing. The woman in red turned her gaze to Desiree and took in a deep breath.

"Desiree Blanc and Jim, that is your name is it not?" Thomas said.

Jim nodded.

"Meet Maggie LeRoux. I love the sound of her name. Maaaggiieee. I intend to name an important character Maggie, I certainly do."

Maggie smiled shyly as she shook Desiree's hand and then Jim's. She looked like a teen-ager, her long dark brown hair worn straight and parted down the center. She had a perfectly symmetrical face with a small, pointy chin and cupie-doll lips painted the same red as her dress. Standing about five-three, she had to look up at both of them.

"Maggie has worked wonders with my love life and she'll work wonders with yours, I am sure. Give them one of your cards, my dear."

Looking slightly embarrassed, Maggie dug a business card from her pocket book and handed it to Desiree who handed it to Jim.

"Would you like to join us for a nightcap?" Thomas offered.

Desiree finally smiled and leaned over to kiss Thomas on the cheek.

"Not tonight. We have a pressing engagement," she said.

"Well." Thomas bowed. "It is always a pleasure to see you." And the two waltzed away, hand in hand.

Desiree shook her head and when they were out of earshot said, "How odd."

Jim looked at the card as they continued down the avenue.

The card read:

Love Sorceress

At The Red Door

Corner Dauphine & St. Philip

dial RAmond-1113

"You're gonna keep the card?" Desiree asked.

He tucked it into his shirt pocket. "I need all the help I can get."

She poked him in the rib again.

• • •

James Gallagher showed up with his moustache on Saturday night, Desiree called Bogarde between shows to get him over early. By Sunday night, her night off, Desiree sat nude on the edge of a bed in a Roosevelt Hotel suite while Bogarde peeked out of the partially closed closet. Both waited for Gallagher to show.

"You're not serious," she'd said Saturday night after getting off and meeting Bogarde, who'd absconded Gallagher for two hours after her last act. "We're really going to try the old cameraman in the closet routine?"

"Yep. Because it'll work. He won't take his eyes off you soon as he gets there because you're going to be naked." Bogarde's eyes lit up. "He'll be all over you and all you have to do is give me a little time to get some good shots?"

"How much time?"

"Until I step out of the closet and show him the camera."

Desiree sat on the bed's edge with her legs crossed, and looked at herself in the dresser mirror. She looked pasty in the bright light. Bogarde needed every light on for the camera. He'd told her about the high-speed black-and-white film that didn't need a flash bulb, but still needed light.

She sat there wondering how she ended up like this. Waiting for a dufus to blackmail. She spent the afternoon with Jim, taking in another matinee, having a quiet dinner after, then telling him a lie that she wasn't feeling well so she could keep this appointment.

What for?

She knew what for – the cold cash sitting in her deposit box, the icy gemstones nestled between the Ben Franklins and U.S. Grants. "This will be the big one," Bogarde had said. "We'll walk out of that bank with fifty, sixty thousand apiece. I guarantee it. And Gallagher can't say a word about it."

Yeah? It couldn't be that easy.

She didn't hear the knock at the door. Bogarde had to lean out of the closet, camera dangling from his neck, to tell her someone was at the door.

"Go. Now!" It came out as a hard whisper and she went to the door.

"Who is it?"

"Me," Gallagher said lightly.

She cracked open the door, looked out with one eye and saw a jittery Gallagher standing there with his fake moustache, perspiration rolling down the sides of his face, his hat in hand, rung like a wet face-rag. She left the door cracked, turned and walked back across the room toward the bed.

She heard the door close behind her and looked over her shoulder at the banker who was staring at her ass as she moved away from him. She let out a deep, sexy laugh and stopped by the bed to arch her back and run her hands through her hair.

Gallagher came up behind her and cupped her breasts in his sweaty hands and she wondered how far Bogarde would let this go. The first snap of the shutter made her flinch and she knew the banker had to have heard, but he was so engrossed with her tits. She managed to ooch them over to the radio and turn it on so the snapping shutter wouldn't be heard.

The only thing that saved her was Gallagher's eagerness to feel up her body and downright clumsiness getting out of his suit. It took a while but he finally got naked and looked pretty pathetic in the bright lights, panting at her and smelling of liquor.

"Oh, Baby." He kept saying, "Oh, Baby."

They were in some pretty compromising positions and it wouldn't be long before he had her where he wanted her. She looked at the closet three times but Bogarde just kept snapping pictures until she finally pushed Gallagher away and said, "Wait. There's someone in the closet!"

"Huh?"

She had to repeat herself as she heard another shutter click. Finally the closet opened and Bogarde stepped out to take one last picture, this one of Desiree standing next to Gallagher, both facing the camera in the buff. She headed for the bathroom to let the men hash it out, let Bogarde put the proposition to Gallagher.

She didn't wait for a ride. She dressed, went down and hailed a taxi, went straight home and took a long, hot bath.

• • •

It was well into the dog days of August, the thirteenth to be exact, an ordinary Wednesday night, when Desiree looked up into her dressing room mirror and saw Alphonso Badalamente standing behind her. In all black, he was nearly invisible in the darkness, except for that wide face. His arms were folded across his chest.

"Oh," she said. "You scared me."

He just stood there looking at her.

She turned slowly and fought the urge to close her robe. She was in costume but felt exposed sitting there. She watched his eyes change slowly, the pupils closing, the brow furrowing.

"You disappoint me," he said in a low voice.

For a moment she thought he maybe talking about her posing with the Negro. Seeing it on film. She'd just got copies from Schroeder and knew they'd all seen them by now. But there was something in Baddie's eyes that told her something different. Something malevolent.

"The beast-and-the-beauty?" he said, shaking his head. "Did you think we wouldn't find out?"

She tried to control her breathing as she looked back into the dark eyes.

"I warned you, didn't I?"

Desiree nodded, her stomach twitching now.

Baddie let out a long sigh. "You know I gotta do something about this."

"I know."

"When you get off later, go by Charity and talk some sense into your boyfriend. If I talk to him he'd end up in the river. Only reason he hasn't is because I don't wanna do the same to you."

Charity Hospital, she thought – Oh, God.

"I gave this some thought the last few days." He leaned against the door. "I was gonna break his pretty face, but I'm gonna give you the choice. Left or right?"

"What?"

"Left arm or right arm. Which one we gonna break. It's your choice."

Desiree felt tears welling and she fought them as hard as she could.

"Left or right?" Baddie's voice even lower now.

"Left."

Baddie stepped over and scooped up her purse, pulling out the Detective Special. "What you need this for?"

"Protection." Her voice quivered and she gritted her teeth.

"Protection? That's what you got me for."

He unloaded the pistol and tossed the bullets on the dressing table. He looked in the barrel. "Your other boyfriend, the bar-back, he teach you how to clean it?"

She couldn't move.

"You took it out shooting didn't you? Got picked up by Sammy?" Baddie closed the chamber and put the pistol on the dressing table. "You remember the rain, don't you?"

She nodded and tried not to recoil as he stepped closer. Baddie reached under her chin and cupped it. He stared into her eyes a long moment before he said. "Your gang days are over. Don't disappoint me again."

She finally blinked as he touched her cheek.

"You know I gotta punish you too."

She couldn't breathe

He walked away. Over his shoulder he added, "I'll think of an appropriate punishment." And he left.

Chapter 11
THAT'S WHY GUYS HAVE MORE HEART ATTACKS

Bogarde felt something was wrong as he stepped into his dark apartment. Someone shoved him hard from behind and he tumbled over the coffee table and landed at the feet of someone sitting on his sofa. The man on the sofa kicked Bogarde on the side of the head and he saw a flash but not in front of his eyes. Behind them. Then the foot came down again, hard and Bogarde heard something snap and he hoped it wasn't his neck. He lay stunned, watching blood from his nose ooze on the carpet.

"Get a fuckin' rag," a harsh voice said.

Footsteps moved toward his kitchen as a pair of strong hands pulled him up in one smooth jerk, sitting him up. Bogarde's eyes were filled with water and he couldn't make out who was there. Wouldn't have been able to in the darkness anyway.

"Here," a different voice said as a wet rag slammed Bogarde's face. "Wipe yourself."

He wiped the blood away, put the rag against his nose and leaned his head back. He felt the two men move to either side and felt each grab an ear and twist.

"Ahhh!"

"Shuddap!" One of them slapped his forehead so hard his head rang like a bell.

They pulled him up by the ears and Bogarde jumped up so quickly he bounced.

"Make a peep and we'll gut you like a tuna."

They held on to his ears and danced him right back out of his apartment and all the way to the street where a third man waited next to a black Packard with the back door open. They shoved him inside and the man with the gravelly voice followed him in. The other went around and got in, while the man who'd been waiting by the car got behind the steering wheel.

By the time they'd crossed Canal, heading toward the warehouse district, Bogarde could see and recognized the driver as Carlo Badalamente. He'd seen the man with the gravelly voice before at Hotsy Jazz. The man was a stump with no neck and wore a turtle-neck shirt. He'd never seen the third man before but the pock-marked face looked subhuman.

"Where are we going?" Bogarde asked and the man with the pock-marked face leaned forward and elbowed Bogarde in the solar plexus. They probably traveled a good three miles before Bogarde could breathe. The car stopped. The men pulled him out. It was then he realized the Packard was a '39 Touring Sedan, in pretty good shape actually.

"Use the door," Carlo said and the man in the turtle neck opened the back door as the pock-marked man spun Bogarde around. Turtle neck rolled down the window while pock-mark shoved Bogarde's left arm though the opening.

It happened so fast he didn't feel it for two long seconds. They used a sledge hammer. He just looked at the ugly fold, the new elbow in his arm and the pain convulsed him. He tried to scream, may have screamed but the agony dropped him like a stone down a well.

He was shoved back into the car for a dizzying ride and felt the bile in his belly rise. He may have barfed but probably didn't because the men didn't hurt him any more. Not that they could with the pain that gripped him, shooting through him like a million razors scraping his nerves. The car turned again and again, accelerated, braked hard, accelerated again until it braked to a stop and he was yanked out, shooting hot coals of pain through his arm.

Bogarde heard the car leave with a screeching of tires. He blinked open his left eye and saw he was face down on blacktop, the smell of blood still in his nose, nauseatingly mixed with the odor of oil and he heard footfalls approaching. White shoes.

A voice said something about a gurney. Someone touched him, tried to roll him and everything went black.

• • •

She rushed past Jim, leaving him with his mouth open as she raced out on Bourbon Street to flag down the first cab she spotted.

"Charity Hospital," Desiree said as she jumped in the back seat. "And hurry."

"You mean step-on-it, right Toots?" The meaty cabbie gave her a salacious grin.

"Fast," she snapped, "and I'm no goddamn toots, you lard-ass!"

The man hit the brakes, turned and she reached for the Detective Special but pulled out some words that worked better. "I work for Badalamente, ass-hole, so hit the gas!"

They ran three stop signs and a red light after the cabbie checked both ways and made it to the Charity Hospital Emergency Room ramp nine minutes after Desiree's last performance of the evening.

She hurried into a wide room filled with folding chairs occupied by people of every color, size and smell. Those not asleep in their chairs stared at her as she ran through them to a nurse sitting at a desk, a police officer in a black uniform, not NOPD, stood next to the desk.

"Abraham Bogarde." She tried to calm her voice. "I'm here to see Abraham Bogarde."

"He not in the waiting room?" asked the prim nurse.

"No." Desiree looked around again. "His arm," she hesitated.

"Ah, the open-compound fracture."

The cop nodded.

"Not often you see someone break their humerus," said the nurse while the cop pointed to is left bicep and ran his finger from his elbow up to his shoulder.

"Are you related to Mr. Bogarde?"

"Girlfriend?"

"And your name?"

"Desiree Blanc."

Eventually, after more questions, the cop, who turned out to be an Orleans Parish Deputy Sheriff, took her into an area marked 'triage' and down a walkway with curtains on either side and the sounds of people moaning or just whimpering. Bogarde lay on a roller bed, his left arm wrapped in a white bandage and resting atop a table up against the bed. His eyes were closed but he was breathing.

A freckle-faced nurse came through the curtain and said, "He's going into surgery. You can follow us upstairs and wait in the waiting room outside the O.R." A huge Negro orderly stepped in and started pulling the bed. The table was attached to the bed and

Bogarde was eased out into the walkway and down to a wide elevator.

Desiree followed, noticing the strong smells now – alcohol, mercurochrome, baby powder. She found a fairly clean chair with a nice cushion against a partially opened window where she could look down on the traffic passing up and down Tulane Avenue while they operated on Bogarde.

You can't die from a broken arm, even if the bone had broken the skin, which Desiree knew happened with an open-compound fracture. At least it was his left arm. She sat with her legs crossed and arms across her chest, all pretzeled up, and waited.

Through her last two performances after Baddie's visit to the dressing room, Desiree could see nothing, not even the faces in the crowd, as she tried not to collapse. The wait was the worst part. Every time she thought of what they'd do to Bogarde, she reminded herself of Baddie's words to her, "You know I gotta punish you too."

Oh, God.

She bent forward and closed her eyes.

Footsteps brought her back and she blinked open her eyes to a pair of feet standing before her, familiar shoes, the left foot twisted.

"You left work?" she asked, not looking up from the feet.

"Couldn't let you do this alone," Jim said as the feet moved away for him to pull a chair closer. "Alphonso Badalamente told me I should come."

She looked up through the tears and said, "Baddie?"

"He sent me. Said you could use a shoulder to lean on maybe."

She didn't want to cry but couldn't stop it. Jim took her in his arms and she shoved her face against his shoulder and let it out. A nurse brought Kleenex and when Desiree got better control of herself, she went to the bathroom to fix her face. By the time she came back out, the crying was gone.

She sat next to Jim and took his hand but he was stiff and distant and said, "You love him, don't you?"

"Nope," she said firmly. "Not at all." She looked at Jim's confused eyes. "I did, a little, when we first started but I wasn't crying because Bogarde got his arm broken."

"You weren't."

"Nope. I was just letting it all out. Sometimes the emotions rise so high, if a girl doesn't let 'em out, we'll explode. That's why guys have more heart attacks."

Now Jim was really confused. He'd always figured women were complicated, but not this complicated. But he knew when to keep his mouth shut and just sit there holding Desiree's hand until the doctor came out. When the doctor came, he seemed to be in a hurry, probably for another operation. He was short and dark haired and spoke with an accent, Indian or Pakistani, as he explained Bogarde would be fine and could go home in a couple days.

"It was good he came here right away, however. Otherwise, he could have lost that arm."

And with that the doctor left.

Desiree leaned against Jim's shoulder and closed her eyes. He closed his and soon they were both breathing deeply, Jim about to doze off, when Desiree said, "We'll see him out of surgery and you'll take me home, OK?"

He nodded.

A few minutes later, he snapped awake.

"What? What is it?" she asked.

"Crater Lake."

"What?"

"I have an army buddy working as a park ranger at Crater Lake, Oregon. Sent me some color pictures and it's gorgeous up there."

She re-snuggled against him. "You wanna be a park ranger?"

He shook his head. "Can't. Not with this foot. But they have bars around Crater Lake and I can bartend now. What I'm saying is we can get away. Make a fresh start."

She snuggled against his shoulder and then went still. Just when he thought she was asleep, she said, "It's not hot up there, is it?"

"Rarely. They have a summer, but there's no humidity."

"Oregon, huh?"

"Southern Oregon. Right above California. Lot closer to Hollywood than here."

• • •

Jim finally got some sleep, but not enough. He woke around eight p.m., wondering where he was for a moment because it was so damn hot. He sat on the edge of his bed, kneading his ankle.

He'd taken Desiree to work at four and she looked pretty tired, but she said the show must go on. He'd gotten a couple hours shut eye. The clock read ten 'till eight at night. He had time, if he took a quick shower so he hobbled to the bathroom to shave.

Just before nine o'clock he arrived at the corner of Dauphine and St. Philip for his appointment and stood looking at the red door of the Creole cottage just across the street from a school playground. Next to the door was a small sign in hand-painted lettering: Sorceress Eros.

He rang the bell and Maggie LeRoux answered immediately. She wore a pink blouse and a red sarong skirt, more a scarlet hue, and her lipstick matched. Her face seemed half-hidden behind her long straight hair, still parted down the center. She opened the door wider and smiled that shy smile.

"Come in, Jim."

He stepped into a living room that was sparsely furnished – a maroon sofa, a tan sofa chair, two end tables with matching brass lamps, all assembled atop a round tan rug on the hardwood floor which shined brightly beneath the lights. A line of candles on the mantle above the fireplace burned, giving off strong, flowery scents.

"Please sit," Maggie said, waving to the sofa as she sat on the chair, tucking her legs under her. She was barefoot. Jim sat and the sofa was too soft. He sank in it.

"Would you like something to drink?"

"No." He had to lean forward to get at his wallet. He pulled out a five and said, "Before I forget."

"We'll get to that," she said as her eyes bored into his. They looked even lighter green, if that was possible and stared at him with that wide-eyed, innocent look again. "You're here because of Desiree."

"I guess I am."

"No guessing about it. She's the one who lights your flame, the one you desire most of all. Apropos with the name 'Desiree'."

"It's not her real name."

Maggie smiled. "It's her soul's name."

She got up, came over and took his hands into hers, which were cool. Those eyes searched his for a few seconds and a smile came to her cupie-doll lips. She went back and sat, tucking her legs again and looked at him and for the second time he had that disarming feeling as he looked back at her.

"You're not from here," she said. "Midwest. No, California, I think. You've traveled a lot." Suddenly the eyes softened and she looked down at the floor. "You were hurt in battle, I'm sure." He watched her take in a few breaths then look up at the sadness was gone from her eyes.

"You will be leaving here soon and you'll be happy."

Jim felt his heartbeat rising. "With her?"

"Oh yes. You'll be traveling and you'll be happy." Maggie stood up and stuck out her hand. "I'll take my fee now."

"That's it?"

"What did you expect? A magic show." She stepped over and took the five. Smiling she looked like a teen-ager again. "I just let you in on the secrets of your heart, your deepest desire. I think you got your money's worth."

She turned and he climbed out of the deep sofa and followed her back to the door. She opened it and before he stepped through it, he asked, "When?"

"Soon," she said and touched his shoulder gently, patting it. "Soon."

There was a strange look on her face and he couldn't tell if it was sad or not.

• • •

After work Desiree was too exhausted to have more than a few sips of club soda, too exhausted to go back to Charity, so she went straight home. She stopped immediately in apartment doorway and stood there looking at the upside down sofa, at the lamps lying on the carpet. She could see the tiny kitchen table was topsy-turvy. Nothing seemed broken, but everything had been turned over. Her bed was in pieces, mattress against one wall, box spring against the other. They'd even checked inside the commode.

Desiree righted one of her two kitchen chairs and sat there wondering if she could just pull the mattress over and crawl atop. Sleep this away and start cleaning up when she had some rest. There was nothing here for them to find. No loot. Then she thought of Mrs. Watson and had to go straight down.

She tapped lightly on the door, hating to wake up her landlady but there was no way she could sleep not knowing Mrs. Watson was all right. The sleepy-eyed old lady peeked out of her door and Desiree sighed.

"You're all right?"

"Why, yes, dear. Are you?"

"Does your nephew still live next door?"

"He does."

"Can he come up tomorrow and help me with the furniture."

Mrs. Watson opened the door and closed her thick robe. "What's wrong with the furniture?"

"It's upside down."

When Mrs. Watson saw what had been done, all she could say was, "How did they do this without me hearing or seeing anything?"

"I'm so sorry," Desiree said. "I told you I work around some unsavory characters." She picked up a sofa cushion.

"Leave it until morning." Mrs. Watson took Desiree's hand. "Come sleep downstairs. I have a spare bedroom."

Desiree wiped the tears from her eyes on the way down. How she'd managed to find someone as nice as Mrs. Watson was a miracle.

"Maybe I should take the deposit box key. They might come back and look for you."

"The key's safe here. They'll never find it. They show back up and I'll bop 'em on the head."

• • •

It wasn't until Friday that Bogarde was released from the hospital. Desiree picked him up in a cab and took him home. She waited as he opened the door, knowing what he'd find and letting him curse as soon as he saw the mess. His left arm wasn't in a sling, but a cast held up by an apparatus around his hip, keeping the arm stuck out, elbow at an angle.

He went straight in to the kitchen and the coffee cans, where he'd stashed his cash, lay tossed around the floor.

"They got it all," he said.

From the kitchen doorway, Desiree told him, "They tossed my place too."

Bogarde looked at his watch. "My sugar mama's coming over. I'll stay with her a while. Thanks for picking me up."

That was it, she guessed. Desiree turned to leave.

"We're gonna score big time with Gallagher," he called out. "And then we'll blow town."

Desiree went back and looked at him. "You serious? Another job?"

His face contorted. "They took everything from us. Just like that." He snapped his right thumb. "Money we got from Elmer and the Roths and the *jewels!*" He took a menacing step toward her but she didn't cringe. "We can't stay in New Orleans. You understand that, don't you?"

She nodded slowly.

He stepped back, took in a long breath and said, "You're my gun-moll, lady. You concentrate on the job ahead and let my heavy-set sugar mama pamper me back to strength."

She felt butterflies fluttering in her belly as she left.

Bogarde went back into the kitchen to the pantry and checked. They hadn't pried open the board. At least he still had the jewels. He got up to get tools, then thought twice. They already missed the jewels. For now, the jewels were safe where they were.

• • •

Late August in New Orleans was hellish with the temperature in triple digits and the humidity hovering around ninety percent. With the Badalamentes in complete control now, Hotsy Jazz was the hottest club around. They put in new air-conditioning, repainted the inside, covered the black walls with tan paint, resurfaced the stage with a shiny hardwood finish and condensed it into a tighter circle to allow more tables. They brightened up the whole place and opened an area at the back of the stage for a live band. A new sign, this one with 'Live JAZZ' was added to the awning above 'Hotsy Jazz! Striptease! Continuous Entertainment!'

The new band leader, an incredibly skinny man named Billy, who looked like a reefer-addict, came up with another number for Desiree, a loud, raucous, jazzy version of Carmen Gray's "Audubon Stroll."

Desiree didn't see Bogarde until after Labor Day. They met at his place and his cast was different, a little smaller and in a sling. He wasn't there to straighten or clean up but to pack up. She helped him fill two suitcases with the clothes he hadn't already brought to his sugar mama's place.

"I've been in contact with Gallagher," he said, tossing socks into a suitcase. "I was gonna set it up for the twelfth. This Friday. But we're gonna need another week getting our plans straight and getting my arm better."

Desiree unpacked his dresser of tee-shirts, shorts and a couple slacks, putting them in a different suitcase.

"I've got Gallagher reeling. He doesn't know what hit him and I *know* this'll work."

"How?"

Bogarde shot her a stern look. "We go in as a couple, just before closing. That's what the employees see. You, as the ditzy blond, insisting on seeing the vault. We go inside and fill up two bags, as much cash as we can carry and we handcuff Gallagher inside and leave him. We just waltz out and they call the cops, of course and describe us. Oh, yeah. You'll need a red wig. They think you're a redhead already."

"Then I'll be a ditzy redhead."

"Yes!" He slammed the suitcase shut. "And Gallagher tells the cops we pulled guns and handcuffed him, told him not to call the police for ten minutes or we'd shoot the employees." Bogarde stepped into his bathroom to clean out the cabinet in there. "The beauty is, he can't tell them who we are because if he does, I told him our lawyer would make sure his wife and the cops and the newspapers get the pictures of you and him and the cops won't believe he wasn't in on the heist."

"So we just leave town."

"Directly. For the airport. I'm getting tickets for Los Angeles. You wanted Hollywood, didn't you? We don't stop. We don't pass

Go. We don't collect our two hundred 'cause we'll have a couple hundred grand."

"That much?"

"Friday the bank stocks cash for business payrolls. The vault's full."

She had that fluttery feeling in her belly again.

• • •

Through the following week, Desiree spent her nights at Hotsy, her days with Jim and her days off planning what to do. She quit shopping for clothes and divided up what she absolutely needed to take with her so she could pack quickly.

She asked Jim about Crater Lake some more, wondering if maybe that would be best, an indirect route to Hollywood. No way she was sticking with Bogarde. She thought he was borderline crazy, desperate to finish the Gallagher job, but the more she thought about the amount of money they'd get the more she warmed to it.

All the while, her stomach never stopped jumping every time something startled her. Baddie didn't look at her much, didn't say anything to her and his men didn't seem to pay her any added attention but she knew she'd have to pay up sooner or later.

"You know I gotta punish you too," he'd said.

Maybe. Just maybe, she could have it all – Gallagher's money – she'd certainly earned it letting him fondle her and slobber over her – the loot she'd accumulated and maybe Jim too. Jim was the problem. Talking him into leaving town would be easy. Staying with him all the way to Oregon would be a breeze, leaving him flat would be hard, maybe the hardest thing she'd ever done.

One of the movies they took in while Desiree waited to be punished was called *A Dandy in Avarice* starring Stewart Granger, Hedy Lamar and creepy Peter Lorre. It wasn't a love triangle because Lorre played the spoiler, the man who kept tripping up the lovers. The dandy dresser, Granger, would do anything for money, swindle anyone, until he met the lovely Lamar who taught him what she'd do for money, which left him standing alone in the cold rain with the police closing in while she drove away with everything they'd swindled.

"I looked up the word," Jim said as they left the Orpheum. "Avarice is an unreasonably strong desire to obtain and keep money."

Desiree felt the hairs standing on the back of her neck.

• • •

It came unexpectedly – Desiree walking from the streetcar on her way to work, a black car pulling up just in front of her and Alphonso Badalamente stepping out of the back seat nodding for her to get in. Turtle drove as Baddie took the Colt from her purse.

They said nothing and Desiree felt her heart beating faster and faster, felt the perspiration in her hands, her throat suddenly parched. They drove to a warehouse and pulled around back. They were in a seedy part of town, but two Cadillacs and a white Ford were parked there.

Baddie got out and she followed, Turtle behind her as they went in.

The place was cool and dark and smelled old, like moldy timbers. Baddie led the way up some stairs to a second floor that was all windows. Bright sunlight filled the room. The place was huge and in the center of the room was a bed with a brass headboard and five men standing around. Schroeder stood next to his camera on a tripod, a second man who could pass for his brother stood holding a sound boom next to a movie camera on a second tripod. The other three men were Negroes. One was Reverend Ardin Clavell in a white suit, the second a middle aged man in a blue suit, the third a tall, young buck, had to be in his early twenties.

"Since you liked to pose with black skin," Baddie said as he and Turtle pulled up stools to sit on. "Your punishment for disobeying me is this." He nodded to Schroeder who took in a deep breath and set up the camera, pointing it at the bed. The man with the movie camera focused his on the bed, then moved the boom over it.

"I don't wanna hear talkin'," Baddie's voice rose and echoed through the wide room. "You can make 'yummy sounds' and go 'ouuu, ahhhh'. The plot's simple. The bucks strip her, she helps them out of their clothes, they pose together and then I'll break out the rubbers."

He pulled a box of condoms from his shirt pocket. "Don't want my girl getting knocked up, Capiche?"

Desiree saw perspiration on the reverend's top lip and the other middle aged man seemed nervous, but not as much as Schroeder. The young Negro didn't look a bit nervous. He just stared at her breasts and waited.

"Start up anytime," Baddie added.

The reverend watched as the two others stripped Desiree, the man in the blue suit unbuttoning her blouse while the young man went around to unzip her skirt. They got her naked and took their clothes off quickly and stood posing next to her before they started touching her. She closed her eyes.

There was a lot of grunting and groaning as the men took her one at a time, then two at a time and she found herself gasping a few times. Her body reacted on its own but she fought the pleasure.

It seemed to go on and on and after the three Negroes were done, Turtle passed her an icy Coke and for a moment she wondered where the hell he'd gotten it. She thanked him and almost smiled until she saw him unzipping his pants. Turtle was gentle at first but the gentleness went away as his passion rose.

Schroeder tried to weasel out of it, telling Baddie he was happily married but Baddie said, "You wanna stay happily married?"

Desiree lay on the bed as Schroeder moved over her. Then it was the sound man's turn.

Turtle brought another Coke but she had to use the bathroom, so he helped her into her shoes and walked with her across the wide floor all the way to a small, stinking bathroom. When she came out, only Baddie was there, still perched on the stool.

She walked straight up to him and said defiantly, "That's it?"

He reached over and fondled her right breast, climbed off the stool and started unbuttoning his shirt.

"Assume the position," he said. She backed up to the bed and crawled backward on it as Baddie took off his clothes and slipped on a rubber. He wasn't gentle until it was over and he lay atop her, kissing her neck.

She waited for him to look in her eyes before she said, "I'm just a whore now."

His hand rose up her neck and he kissed her lips. "Not completely," he said. "You're just a whore this afternoon." He rolled off her. "Disappoint me again and I'll put you in one of our houses and you'll see what it's like to be one of our whores."

The fuck he was saying. She'd just seen it.

• • •

They took her home and Baddie put a hundred dollars in her purse, along with her gun.

"For the tips you missed tonight," he said as she climbed out.

Mrs. Watson opened her door and asked if she were all right. Desiree nodded but wouldn't look at the old woman and couldn't get up the stairs quickly enough. She couldn't climb in the tub fast enough either and sat in it as it filled. She thought she would cry but it wouldn't come. She'd been used by seven men and what sickened her was – it felt good, or pleasurable at least. That disgusted her most of all.

She called Jim before he left for work and asked him to call in sick. "Tell Leo that Alphonso Badalamente knows why and come over, will you?"

"I'll be right there."

She put on a blouse and Capri pants and met him at the door with a cold beer. They kissed once and she pulled him to the sofa. Soft music echoed from her Victrola and she said she just wanted to snuggle.

"Are you all right?"

She nodded as she put her head against his chest. No way she could ever tell him what happened.

"Tell me about Oregon again," she said.

"I've been reading up on it," he said. "They say the air is so clean and fresh and the water is sparkling right out of the faucet."

• • •

Desiree and Jim were off Friday and Saturday, that was a week before Bogarde's planned bank heist. Jim thought they'd take in some matinees. Desiree packed, getting everything she'd take to Hollywood, via Oregon, in three suitcases and a make-up case.

"We'll need a car," she told Jim as they walked up Canal Street for the Saenger on Friday afternoon.

"I have some money saved," Jim said.

"So do I.

"Leo knows a car dealer. Not your friend, of course."

She bumped his hip with hers and said, "No. No car dealer. We have to buy one from an original owner. Someone advertising in the paper. You haven't mentioned Oregon to Leo, have you?"

"No."

"Good. Don't tell anyone anything. We have to make a clean break."

Jim pulled out his wallet to buy the tickets as they arrived. "When are we making this break?"

"Next Friday. I'll tell you all about it after the flick."

She didn't think she'd be paying much attention to the movie but two minutes into *The Ghost and Mrs. Muir* and she was as far away from her thoughts and troubles as possible. It was captivating, the romance between head-strong and independent Mrs. Muir, Gene Tierney at her best, and the head-strong and independent ghost of the sea captain played by British actor Rex Harrison. Their love was all emotion, all intellect, no carnality and that warmed Desiree.

What captured her attention even more was Gull Cottage, the sea-side house Mrs. Muir rented and the ghost haunted. It looked spooky and homey at the same time, an isolated wind-swept place near the beach and yet warm and comfortable inside.

"Pretty good movie," Jim said as they left the Saenger, a few minutes after Rex Harrison led the spirit of Mrs. Muir away.

"Gull Cottage," said Desiree. "You think we could find a place like that? I mean, along the Oregon coast?"

"Crater Lake isn't on the coast but there's a lot of coast in Oregon."

Desiree snuggled with Jim as they walked. "I love the way he called her, 'ma dear'."

"I have a map at home," he said. "We can see what towns are on the coast."

They went over the map and she went over the instructions.

"Meet you at the airport?"

"I'll call you when to come and you meet me at the passenger departure area. Delta Airlines."

• • •

On Saturday, they bought a two-door, '37 Plymouth coupe. It was in excellent condition. They bought it from the wife of the director of the New Orleans boat harbor. The family was going to give it to their son when he started LSU but decided on getting him a new car. Jim was excited because the car had new tires and only 32,000 miles.

"She didn't dog it, that's for sure."

All Desiree noticed was the odd placement of the windshield wipers attached to the top of the windshield, instead of the bottom. They made love that evening but Desiree couldn't get into it. She knew she'd come out of the depression she'd felt since Baddie whored her out, but it would take time.

Desiree Blanc had made up her mind to leave the day she went upstairs with Mrs. Watson's nephew to straighten up her place. She'd made up her mind to do the bank heist the night Badalamente whored her out.

She dug the Detective Special from her purse, unloaded it and dry-fired it again and again, double action, then cocking the hammer to squeeze the trigger single-action. If they came for her again, she'd use it. If they tried to stop her, she'd use it. If she and Jim didn't get away, they'd have to kill her. She pointed the gun at her dresser mirror and squeezed the trigger as the hammer fell, again and again. Desiree was prepared, in her heart, to show them what a gun-moll could do.

On Wednesday, September 17th, she paid her October rent in advance. Only way she could think of paying Mrs. Watson back. Mrs. Watson suspected something was up, she was sure, especially when Desiree retrieved her deposit box key.

Desiree kept checking her bags and made a list of what to do. On Thursday, she went to the bank and got her money and jewels, brought them to Jim and told him they were leaving town the next day.

"Tomorrow, for sure?"

"For sure."

She held his right hand in both of hers and looked into those deep brown eyes. "I've something to show you." She opened the big purse she'd brought and pulled out the cash and the gems, each set of stones in a separate envelope, and laid out the loot on his coffee table.

"My God," he gasped.

Minus the two hundred she'd chipped in for the Plymouth and the money she'd spent on Canal Street or sent home, Desiree had forty-five hundred in cash and all the gems from Roth Brothers.

"This will start our new life," she said and meant it.

"More than that." Jim looked from the loot to her and then back again. He took in a deep breath and said, "You have to tell me how you got this."

She took his hand again and started with Elmer from Topeka.

That night, as they both lay in bed, neither able to sleep, Desiree told herself *money* was more important than seeing her face on the big screen. It meant not going hungry again, not worrying about how to live. Hollywood may come later, when the heat died down and Baddie no longer looking for her.

She sat up and told Jim, no, don't meet her at the airport. "I want you to meet me outside the bank. I'll jump in your car instead of Bogarde's."

Jim sighed heavily. "What bank?"

Chapter 12
WHAT ELSE CAN I DO

On the last day he'd ever spend in New Orleans, Jim sat on his bed and looked around his room. He'd packed what he'd take, including the newest issues of *Planet Stories, Amazing Stories* and *Astounding*. His two suitcases, along with Desiree's sat in his bedroom, the money and gems divided among each bag.

Their map lay on the kitchen table with two routes marked out, both to Houston where they'd decide to go the north route or the south. North took them through Denver and Salt Lake City. South took them through San Antonio, El Paso and over to Tucson and Los Angeles before going straight up the coast to Oregon. The southern route was longer, but they'd get to see California.

Jim folded the map and poured himself another cup of coffee. He'd gone out for beignets – he would miss them – and picked up the *Santa Fe Pueblo* and two local newspapers, the *States* and the *Item* earlier and decided he might as well read them now as he waited. Headlines on all three papers was about the hurricane that ravaged Fort Lauderdale. The damn thing crossed Florida and ended up in the Gulf of Mexico where it was re-strengthening and heading directly for New Orleans.

There were pictures of destroyed houses, overturned boats and wires dangling from bent telephone poles. The hurricane had made landfall just south of a place called Hillsboro Beach on the Atlantic side of Florida. Waves pounding the seawall at Miami dwarfed one story houses. Hurricane-force winds extended a hundred and twenty miles from the eye. A storm surge of eleven feet inundated beachside properties. It was slow moving and dumped a prodigious amount of rain over the area, causing severe flooding away from the shore. It crossed over Sanibel Island as it went out into the gulf and would probably make landfall near New Orleans Friday evening. It was late morning Friday and the sky was bright blue and clear.

Why the hell hadn't he and Desiree heard about this storm?

Because they hadn't listened to the radio and he hadn't bought a newspaper for days. He and Desiree were hunkered down in his place and no one, not one fool, mentioned it at Hotsy Jazz, not even Leo. He and Leo had talked about hurricanes once, but Leo said no storm was powerful enough to do much damage to New Orleans because the Gulf of Mexico was a hundred miles away.

"What about the lakes?" Jim had asked.

"Too shallow," was the answer.

There was nothing in the papers about Roswell. At one p.m., Jim looked out his window and had to go outside to make sure he wasn't hallucinating. The sky to the west and north was still bright and clear but the sky to the south and east was dark and angry, battleship gray changing to charcoal gray and pitch back in the distance.

The damn thing was coming and Desiree was heading for the bank in forty-five minutes.

• • •

"What hurricane?" Desiree asked as she climbed into Bogarde's Ford.

"The one that hit Fort Lauderdale. Son-of-a-bitch is almost here."

The traffic was heavy and she spotted men boarding up windows as they turned on to Rampart Street.

"Nice wig," Bogarde said, then hit the horn at a slow-moving truck took its time turning off the street.

Desiree hadn't paid much for the wig but it wasn't a bad one, curly. She'd look like Little Orphan Annie if she wasn't in a tight purple dress. She spent even less on the two beat-up suitcases she'd picked up at the Salvation Army, cases she tossed in the trunk when Bogarde pulled up. They were empty but she knew Bogarde wouldn't get out of the car to help her, so he'd never know her real bags were with Jim.

"You think the bank might close early?" She asked as she saw businesses already closed.

"Better goddamn not!"

As they crossed Canal Street, Desiree unbuttoned the top buttons of her dress all the way to her bra, then unbutton the bottom buttons up to her stocking tops.

"What're you doing?"

"If they have a bank guard or any male tellers, they won't even see my face."

Bogarde gunned the Ford and ran through a light just turning red. There was a prowl car sitting at the intersection and Desiree held her breath, waiting for the inevitable siren, but it didn't come.

No use correcting Bogarde, he'd probably explode. He was having trouble driving with one arm. She'd suggested letting her drive, although she wasn't very good at it, but he gave her the old line about women drivers, so she let him. Like their Plymouth, Bogarde's Ford was an automatic so she shifting gears wasn't a problem.

They finally got to the bank and found a parking place right in front, two cars in front of where Jim sat in the Plymouth. Desiree jumped out and looked back at Jim, giving him a long stare, before she followed Bogarde into the bank. A gust of wind flapped her dress as she entered and it caught the attention of the bank guard right away. Must have got a glimpse of stocking tops, maybe a hint of panties.

She wrapped her arm around Bogarde and slowed him down as they walked straight up to James Gallagher who looked like he was closing up his office.

"Remember us?" Bogarde said.

She thought Gallagher would faint.

"We've come to open that account," said Bogarde as another bank officer looked at them. "The little woman's worried. She'd like to see the vault." Bogarde chuckled nervously. "She wants to see how thick the walls are."

"Um," Gallagher said as he stood up. "Oh, yes." He turned to the other officer. "Sam, finish the close-down. I'll only be a few minutes."

On their way to the vault, Gallagher called out to the guard. "You can shut the door. We'll be leaving after these clients."

The guard waved and went to the door.

Soon as they stepped into the vault, past two barred gates, Bogarde took a pair of handcuffs out of the bag he carried, while Desiree took her bag off her shoulder. Without a word, Gallagher went to a row of stainless steel lockers, took out a key and unlocked them. Inside were stacks of new money.

"Used bills," Bogarde growled.

"Oh. Yes. Yes." Gallagher opened a second locker and there were neat stacks of bills wrapped in wrappers, used bills. Desiree and Bogarde stuffed their bags. They had Gallagher open a third locker and Desiree had trouble picking up her bag once it was filled. Bogarde had Gallagher help him put his bag on his shoulder, then handcuffed Gallagher to the inner gate.

"Not a goddamn word!" Bogarde snarled.

They went out as casually as possible, noticing all the tellers and Sam, the other officer, were busy putting things away. The guard watched them approach but didn't seem to even notice they were weighed down by the bags as he looked at Desiree's legs. She reached down to tug on a stocking, showing some panty now, for certain.

"Thank you," she purred as the guard opened the door for them, let them out.

Bogarde looked back and told the guard, "We're the 'beauty-and-the-beast'. Remember that."

The guard looked confused, shrugged then locked the door as they stepped away into blustery wind whipping down the street.

They hurried to the Ford, Desiree walking past to Jim who was out now and approaching her. Bogarde threw his bag into the trunk, turned and saw Desiree pass her bag to Jim. Bogarde stood frozen, a stunned look on his face. He kept blinking as if his brain was unable to register the vision of Desiree climbing into the car with Jim. She pulled off her wig as they drove by and took a quick turn off Poydras to head for Tulane Avenue and the way west.

They didn't speak. Desiree scrunched over to sit close to Jim, putting her arm around his neck as they meandered through traffic. Both lanes were pretty jammed, so were the two lanes going back downtown. The rain started by the time they reached Jefferson Davis Parkway, heavy rain that slapped the windshield. Jim slowed with the other cars.

When they reached Carrollton, a horn blowing behind them turned Desiree around to see Bogarde right on their tail.

"Jesus!"

"He's been behind us for a couple blocks," Jim said through gritted teeth.

She saw the Ford cut into the right lane and accelerate, riding next to them now on the four-lane street. Through the rainy window she saw Bogarde glaring at her, mouthing words she was glad she couldn't hear. He hit the gas and the Ford almost hit the car in front of it but Bogarde managed to cut in front of their Plymouth. Jim eased off on the accelerator as Bogarde sped ahead.

"Thought he was going to jam the brakes," Jim said.

Another car zoomed past them on the right, a gray DeSoto driven by a man with dark hair and Desiree thought it was the same damn DeSoto she'd seen in the quarter, but the car took the next right and she let out a sigh. She'd been so paranoid, she was seeing detectives when there were none around.

Then she spotted a black car with two men zip past and pull in behind Bogarde's Ford. One of the men in the black car looked like Turtle. She gasped and reached for the Detective Special in her purse.

"What?" Jim said.

"Car right in front of us. I think Turtle's in there."

The traffic grew denser and the cars slowed to a crawl. The car in front was a Packard and Jim saw two heads. As they took the overpass over the railroad yard, Jim saw Bogarde's Ford right in front of the Packard.

"He's still heading for the airport," Jim said.

"Do planes fly in this kind of weather?"

Jim reached turned on the radio.

" … over eleven feet of water at Shell Beach. We have a report from Bay St. Louis, Mississippi here." The sound of rustling paper came over the radio, followed by, "Over eleven feet of water over the seawall at Bay St. Louis. The big problem along the coast is the rising water from the gulf, but the wind here in the city will get a lot worse and soon.

"We're expecting sustained winds of over a hundred miles and hour to hit the city in the next few hours. The eye is projected to cross right over New Orleans. This is a bad one folks. Those in Gentilly and especially in Jefferson Parish are in for major flooding. Lake Pontchartrain is reclaiming the land."

They were on Airline Highway now, in Jefferson Parish but no flooding yet. Desiree didn't know how far the lake was from

Airline Highway but she felt a little better as the rain seemed to let up somewhat and better yet when the radio announcer said Airline was the designated hurricane evacuation route.

"Do you think he's just heading west, like us, or is he still heading for the airport?"

Jim shrugged and dropped back for a red car to slip in between then and the Packard. "Maybe he's not listening to the radio."

"Do you think they saw us come out of the bank?"

Jim looked at her. "God, I hope not."

"Then how'd they find Bogarde?" She realized and said it aloud. "They must have been following us."

Jim nodded and slowed more but no one cut in front of him. Behind him a horn started blowing so he picked up speed to get close to the red car again.

"If they did, then they'll be looking for you too."

"I know."

She watched his face grow tight and he took in a deep breath and said, "There's only one way to do this."

When he didn't go on, she said, "How?"

"Stick with them and when they jump what's his name, we'll ambush them. Those are the only two who saw you." Jim looked at her. "My Luger's loaded and you've got your gun, right?"

She nodded slowly.

"Hopefully, they won't see us coming." A moment later he added, "If they do, they won't expect us to come gunning." Jim's voice was deeper, more solid and Desiree knew he meant every word.

The traffic didn't thin out but the red car turned into a filling station, which was jam packed, and the cars ahead picked up speed as the rain picked up. Desiree wasn't sure where the airport was exactly but the rain seemed to slacken as she spotted a street sign that read: Williams. The streetlights went out, so the did traffic lights and everyone slowed.

She looked around and all the electricity was out now and it was dark as night. Jim nodded to the right as their headlights picked up a large white sign with blue lettering: Moisant Air Field.

"It's flooded," Desiree said. The lights were still on at the airport and with the rain letting up she saw a wide swatch of water, like a lake, spread from Airline Highway across the flat plain of the airport. Two airplanes on the tarmac had water half-way up their wheels.

"He's turning off," Jim said. Up ahead Bogarde's Ford turned right at the airport entrance, water flying from his wheels as he hit deeper water. The Packard pulled behind and the Ford stopped.

Jim pulled the Plymouth to the shoulder and stopped. Through the rain, Desiree saw the Packard stop behind the Ford and saw both doors open just as Jim opened his door. She fumbled with her purse for the Detective Special, managing to get it out as Jim came around the front of their car. She opened her door to the sharp sound of gunfire and saw the flashes on either side of Bogarde's Ford.

Jim looked back and her, came back and took her hand, drawing her forward to the rear of the Packard. They were hunched down in water over their ankles. He had his Luger in both hands and she raised and cocked her pistol. He nodded and moved up the side of the car, keeping down.

They had to keep wiping the rain from their eyes as they peeked out. Desiree saw one man leaning in the front passenger door of the Ford, the other man opening the trunk and reaching inside for the suitcases.

"Cover me," Jim said. "I'm going after the man leaning in the car."

She tried leveling the Detective Special at Turtle's back as he yanked one of her empty suitcases out of the trunk but she had to wipe the rain from her eyes, so she held her gun with one hand. Jim moved quickly, bouncing with his limp and moving out to get a clear shot at the man just emerging from the passenger side. Jim fired once and she saw the bullet strike the man's side and Jim fired four more rounds quickly.

Desiree looked back at Turtle who was turning toward Jim with a big automatic in his hand. She squeezed her trigger and the Colt kicked and she missed. Jim and Turtle and Desiree fired together and Desiree kept firing until her gun was empty, sure that some of the rounds hit Turtle, who flinched with the strike of the bullets. He seemed to go up on his toes as his gun dropped and he reached for his belly. He flopped against the trunk and bounced forward, face first in the water and didn't move.

Jim came around, grabbed the money bag from the Ford's trunk and came back to her, taking her hand and pulling her to the Plymouth. He was limping more now and surprised her by going to the passenger side. He turned and said, "You drive!"

He had the Luger pressed against his side and she saw blood. He tossed Bogarde's money bag into the back seat, climbed in and slammed the door. The rain slapped Desiree as she went around and jumped in. She'd lost her left shoe. A car had pulled over behind them and a man was leaning out the window and yelling something.

She waved him away. It took several long seconds to crank up the engine with her hands shivering, and she had to start it again but got the Plymouth going. She was almost side-swiped as she pulled into traffic but gunned the engine and the car lurched forward. Jim held on to the dashboard with his right hand and she looked down at his left. The blood hadn't gotten any worse.

"Where's the nearest hospital?"

He shook his head and nodded for them to go on. "Let's go! Let's go." He looked behind them. "Keep heading west. "

It took all her strength to keep the car on the road with the water rising and in the minutes that followed, she was sure they'd stall a couple times. Two cars did, both in the left lane. She stuck to the right and felt the car floating through deeper areas but soon the highway had no standing water and the pace increased.

She frantically wiped the rain from her face and looked at Jim again. He leaned against the door and watched her. He smiled. Her teeth chattered as she said, "How do you feel?"

He nodded, reached over and turned on the heater. He leaned back again and gritted his teeth. "Just keep driving."

She had to watch the road as the Plymouth got up to forty miles and hour now.

"The pain's not bad," he said a minute later. "Burned like hell at first. But, uh, it'll be OK."

"There has to be a hospital around here."

"Baton Rouge," he said. "Just get us to Baton Rouge."

Desiree gunned it and the car accelerated through the rain. It was pitch on either side of the highway. She focused straight ahead and followed the taillights of the cars in front of her.

"How far is Baton Rouge?"

"Seventy. Eighty miles. Just keep going."

It hit her then. Jesus, they'd killed Turtle and who else? It wasn't either Badalamente, maybe the new man with the pockmarked face. They'd find Bogarde's body but not hers. Would they go after her?

She held tightly to the steering wheel and wished the miles away.

By the time she spotted the Baton Rouge city limits sign, Jim was dozing. She could see him breathing and hoped he was asleep and not unconscious. She had to tap the brakes for a slow-moving truck and Jim's eyes snapped open. He sat up, looked down at his wound and asked where they were.

"Baton Rouge."

"Don't stop here."

"What? You've got a bullet in you."

He smiled at her again and looked paler. "It didn't hit any vital organ. This is too big a town. They're small towns just on the other side, right across the river."

Traffic was surprisingly light in the city and the rain slackened a great deal by the time she got on the Huey P. Long Bridge over the river. It was a railroad bridge and pretty narrow for cars but Desiree was glad she couldn't see the river below because the damn bridge was so high she wondered when she'd start the decent.

"We have to find a hospital," she said as they reached the ground on the west side of the Mississippi.

Jim nodded and closed his eyes again. "I been … thinking about … uh … Gull Cottage again. Oregon coast."

"Me too," she said, gripping the steering wheel even tighter and looking around at the darkness. "You said small towns just past Baton Rouge." She didn't see any.

They passed a motel that was dark, except one light in what looked like the office. She went a couple more miles and sped up. Jim was looking out the window now, wiped it with his right hand.

"Fishing camps," he said and sure enough there were camps perched on pilings to their right next to some sorta lake. A couple of the camps had lights on their porches, lights that were *lit*.

When she looked back at Jim, she saw blood on his lips.

"A phone! We gotta find a phone!" She pumped the brakes and spotted a larger camp off to the right with lights on the porch. She slowed even more and crept to the driveway and through the open gate. There was a shell drive up to the camp and places to park under, so she pulled the Plymouth under the camp, killed the engine and climbed out.

She danced barefoot over the shells to the stairs and hurried up them, her Detective Special in hand. The place was locked but the front door had glass panes. She knocked twice, then slammed the Colt against the pane near the door knob and it shattered. She reached in and unlocked the door, letting it fall open and went back for Jim.

She found him at the bottom of the stairs, looking up at her and trying to climb up.

"Wait! Wait!" She hurried down, wrapped his right arm over her shoulder and helped him up the stairs. The only light that worked in the place was the damn porch light. She flipped on switches on their way through the wide front room, Jim weighing her down.

A lamp next to a sofa didn't work either. She moved to help Jim to the sofa but he shook his head, pulled away and walked to a glass door leading to a covered back porch. He went out and sat on a bench, his back against the wall. The wind blew in through the screens in gusts, then fell away to return a few moments later.

"Need … air," he gasped.

Desiree made sure he was comfortable and went back into the stuffy camp. It smelled like it hadn't been opened in a while and she panicked, wondering if it even had a phone. It did, on a small kitchen counter. She picked it up and there was a dial tone. She looked at the number in the center ring of the phone and dialed the operator. Nothing. She waited. Turning on the tap, she wet a dish rag, put the receiver on the counter next to the phone and ran out to wipe Jim's lips.

"Want some water?"

He nodded.

She went back in, checked the receiver then filled a glass with tap water, rinsing the glass first. She tasted it and it didn't taste bad. She checked the receiver again before bringing the water to Jim. He was sitting up more and she held the glass to his mouth and he drank it all.

Desiree hurried back for the phone. Hung up and dialed the operator again. No answer. She felt the seconds ticking with her heartbeat. When she tried the operator a third time, the line was dead. She hung up slowly and the lights went out, the rain letting increasing now.

She went back on the porch and Jim said, "We'll wait it out here." The wind blew across them, damp with rain. She sat next to Jim, wrapped her arms around him and pulled him close.

He pointed to the lake as lightning danced in the distance, illuminating the black water.

"Pretty," He said.

She nodded.

"I love you, Desiree."

She pressed her face against his chest and nodded again.

"It's Dorothy," she said, her voice breaking. "Just plain Dorothy Jellnick from hick Mississippi."

He shook his head. "No. You're Desiree. My Desiree."

She raised her head and kissed his lips lightly before pressing her head against his chest again. A moment later Jim chuckled.

"What's funny about this?"

"She said I'd travel and be happy."

"Who?"

"The Love Sorceress."

She pulled up and looked at his eyes. "You saw her?"

He smiled wanly, looking even paler. "Went to see … our future. She said … I'd travel and … be happy." He blinked tears from his eyes, lips quivering as he tried to smile again. "She … didn't say … how long it'd last."

They kissed again and she put her head against his chest, this time listening for his heartbeat. His breathing seemed a little easier, less raspy.

"Not ... exactly ... Gull Cottage ... ma dear." His chest rose and fell and she closed her eyes and lay there and felt herself slipping away, drifting to sleep until she realized he'd stopped breathing. Desiree pulled away, wiping tears from her eyes and Jim's eyes were half open as if he was still staring out at the water.

"Jim? Jim?" she picked up his limp right hand and searched for a pulse. She pressed her ear against his chest but his chest was quiet now. She cried and held him tightly, unable to stop the tears. She held him until the warmth was gone from his body. For hours.

Sitting up stiffly, she realized the wind had died down and a faint light glowed over the water. Could it be the dawn? Could it be a new day? Desiree stood on wobbly legs and knew she had to get a hold of herself. She had to. It was then she saw how much blood had pooled beneath the bench.

She felt dizzy, moved back and held on to the arm of the bench. Her arms ached, her legs throbbed and her feet felt as if she were standing on hot coals. It took a minute for her to push away from the bench and longer to get into the kitchen where she filled another glass with water and drank it down without stopping. She drank another, wiped her mouth and went down to the car.

She dug out a pair of Capri pants, blouse and underwear and a pair of white tennis shoes she'd never worn yet. She left her make-up case in the car and tried to hurry back up the stairs, having to hold on to the rail to get up. Changing quickly, she washed the make-up from her face and went back out to see Jim one more time.

Desiree held his face in both hands and told him what she should have told him when he could hear her.

"I loved you Jim, more than I've loved anyone and I'm so sorry. What I did to you. I'm so sorry, honey." Tears fell on Jim's chest as she spoke, the words choking off. She kissed his cold lips. "I'm going to find Gull Cottage." Her heart ached. "Will you meet me there?"

She rose slowly, touched Jim's lips with her fingers one last time and went down to their Plymouth. She got behind the wheel and reloaded the Detective Special. If the bastards came for her, she'd gun 'em down because she *was* a gun-moll.

Desiree left the body of her war hero on the porch of some camp just west of Baton Rouge. As she pulled back on the highway, she thought of the bags in the trunk, bags filled with money and jewels and the possibility of a future without the poverty of her past.

The End

Note from the Publisher
BIG KISS PRODUCTIONS

If you found a typo or two in the book, please don't hold it against us. We are a small group of volunteers dedicated to presenting quality fiction from writers with genuine talent. We tried to make this book as perfect as possible, but we are human and make mistakes.

BIG KISS PRODUCTIONS and the author are proud to sell this book at as low a cost as possible. Even ***great*** fiction should be affordable.

Also by the Author

Novels

Battle Kiss
Enamored
John Raven Beau
Slick Time
Mafia Aphrodite
The Big Show
Crescent City Kills
Blue Orleans
The Big Kiss
Grim Reaper

Short Story Collections

New Orleans Confidential
New Orleans Prime Evil
New Orleans Nocturnal
New Orleans Mysteries
New Orleans Irresistible

Hollow Point & The Mystery of Rochelle Marais
LaStanza: New Orleans Police Stories
Backwash of the Milky Way

Screenplay

Waiting for Alaina

Non-Fiction

A Short Guide to Writing and Selling Fiction
Specific Intent

•

For more information about the author go to
http://www.oneildenoux.net

"O'Neil De Noux ... No one writes New Orleans as well as he does." James Sallis

"… the author knows his stuff when it comes to the Big Easy." *Publisher's Weekly*, 3/13/06

O'Neil De Noux would like to hear from you. If you liked this book or have ANY comment, email him at denoux3124@yahoo.com

OTHER BOOKS by De Noux
http://www.oneildenoux.net

BATTLE KISS
THE BATTLE OF NEW ORLEANS
a novel
O'NEIL De NOUX
Daria

John Raven Beau
a novel
O'Neil De Noux

O'NEIL DE NOUX
a sexy caper
Slick Time

New Orleans
Confidential
O'Neil De Noux
Introduction by
James Sallis

O'NEIL DE NOUX
a crime novel
Enamored

New Orleans
Mysteries
O'Neil De Noux

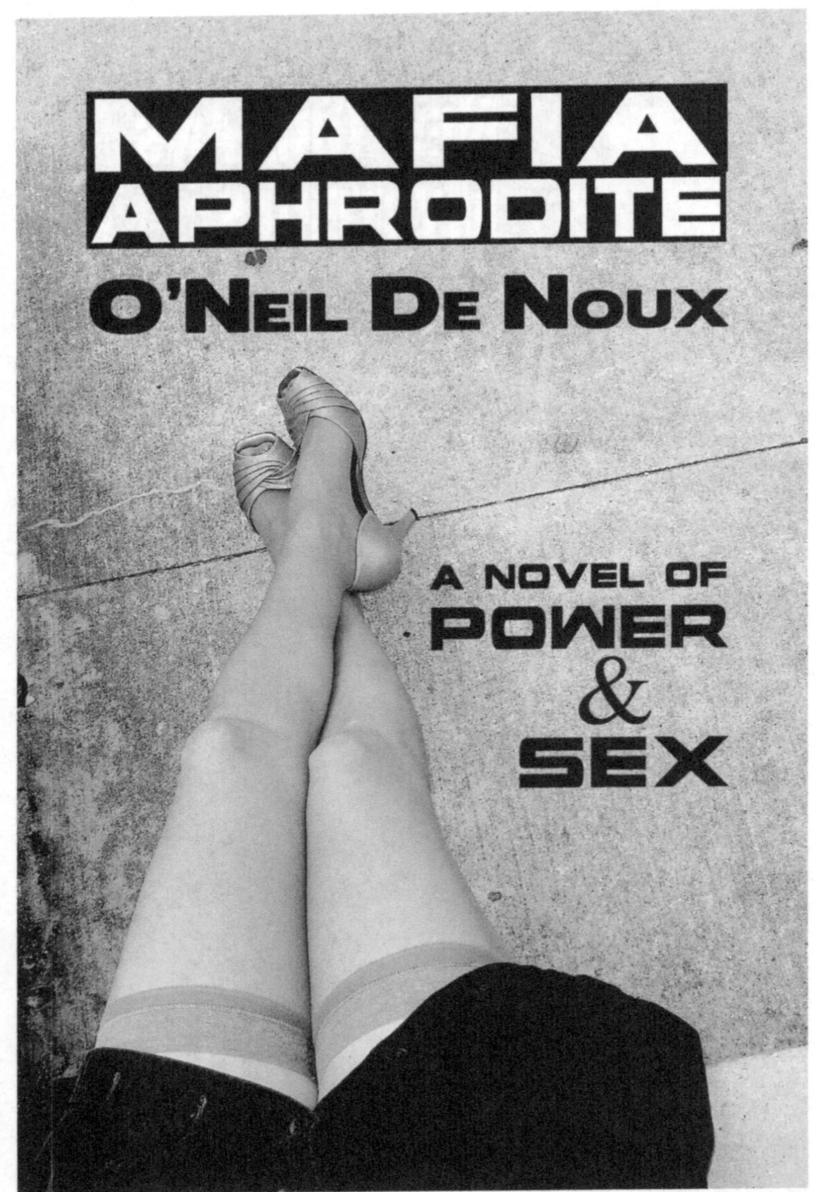
MAFIA
APHRODITE
O'Neil De Noux
A NOVEL OF
POWER
&
SEX

Made in the USA
Las Vegas, NV
12 October 2024

96742804R00108